# Ransom for the Stars
## *the Last Supra*

### By

# Jim Bray

**PublishAmerica
Baltimore**

© 2005 by Jim Bray.
All rights reserved. No part of this book may be reproduced, stored in a retrieval system or transmitted in any form or by any means without the prior written permission of the publishers, except by a reviewer who may quote brief passages in a review to be printed in a newspaper, magazine or journal.

First printing

At the specific preference of the author, PublishAmerica allowed this work to remain exactly as the author intended, verbatim, without editorial input.

ISBN: 1-4137-7627-2
PUBLISHED BY PUBLISHAMERICA, LLLP
www.publishamerica.com
Baltimore

Printed in the United States of America

*To my beautiful wife, Marianne,
who has always been there for me
and for whom I will always be there as well.*

Blair,
Thanks for being a good friend.
You had it took ur so long!
Let's keep in touch!
braj@technofico.com

# Acknowledgements

I would like to uncork a bottle of Ramallan Rainbow wine and propose a toast to:
My father, Jack Bray and my late mother, Margaret, for their love, encouragement, and for being role models.
My sons, Christopher and Johnny, for giving me a reason to be a role model.
My family and friends for their support and kindness.

Mirella Patzer, author, for her friendship, advice, and help.
Special thanks to Sheilagh Price for her editorial help and friendship.
Ingrid Holst, photographer and compatriot, for making my face look not too frightening to be displayed on a book cover.

And, by no means least, to the giants of science fiction, action adventure, and fantasy literature, movies, and TV, who broadened my horizons, entertained me mightily, and inspired me to write this story.

# Contents

| | |
|---|---:|
| AN EBONY ENEMY -- Chapter 1 | 7 |
| VACATED VACATION -- Chapter 2 | 16 |
| AUNTIE'S ESTABLISHMENT -- Chapter 3 | 25 |
| BACK IN THE SADDLE AGAIN -- Chapter 4 | 35 |
| DERELICT DUTY -- Chapter 5 | 46 |
| XANNYK PANIC -- Chapter 6 | 55 |
| RUMINATIONS AND CALCULATIONS -- Chapter 7 | 64 |
| A FRIEND INDEED -- Chapter 8 | 72 |
| SNEAKING A PEEK -- Chapter 9 | 83 |
| ON THE RUN -- Chapter 10 | 95 |
| ELBOW BENDING -- Chapter 11 | 106 |
| EXCURSION FOR CONVERSION -- Chapter 12 | 116 |
| STOREBOUGHT INFORMATION -- Chapter 13 | 128 |
| TADDAYOOSH -- Chapter 14 | 138 |
| MAKTEER -- Chapter 15 | 149 |
| INTO THE VOID -- Chapter 16 | 160 |

PUSH COMES TO SHOVE -- Chapter 17     169

MISSION ACCOMPLISHED -- Chapter 18     184

# AN EBONY ENEMY -- Chapter 1

Grriyll was whistling, if anyone of human descent could have thought that of such gawd-awful twittering, when the computer hooted for attention.

"Hey Grriyll, knock it off, will ya?" To her left Jock Braeden, who'd been sprawled comfortably in his chair by the communications panel, leaned forward to shut off the damn klaxon. Grriyll stopped the wheezing twittering racket.

"Why does music bother you so much, human?"

"It's not music, I mind, Grriyll, it's that damn whistling."

Grriyll would have given Braeden a firm blow to his temple, but duty called. She put the discussion on hold and turned to face the screen. It was covered with its familiar, ever-changing mass of mathematics. Grriyll leaned in closer. After a moment she said, "A ship is coming out of hyperspace beside us."

"Huh? That's nuts."

"Be that as it may," she wheezed, "It is a ship." She waved an appendage in the direction of her screen as if that proved everything, which, of course, it usually did.

"No, no...never mind." Braeden shut up. Grriyll not only couldn't whistle, but she had no sense of humor, either. If she weren't so damn good at her job she'd be useless. Braeden went over to the viewport. "Holy cow!" He shook his head. "What gives?"

"Call the Captain."

"Huh? Oh, yeah." He thumbed the intercom button. "Captain Grant to the Bridge. Captain Grant to the Bridge."

Near enough to the liner that its size could be estimated with the naked eye, a large, black-painted ship had popped into normal space on what looked like a collision course with H.V. QUEEN VICTORIA. It was so black as to be almost invisible and indeed, were it not for the stars it eclipsed, it would have been quite difficult for the untrained eye to see without instruments.

It showed up loud and clear on the scanner, though, and Grriyll touched her suckers to pad after pad on the console, trying to identify the ship. Pictures of the many models of spaceship in Central Registry flashed on the screen beside a sensor data image of the intruder, as Grriyll and the computer checked them for a match. It came within seconds.

"It is a Class IV freighter," Grriyll said as the picture of the ship outside overlaid itself onto one in the records.

Except that it was impossible.

"Don't be ridiculous. They don't do hyperspace!" Braeden stated what should have been obvious to both Grriyll and the computer, neither of which he thought were nearly as fallible as they gave themselves credit for.

"I report the truth," Grriyll said shortly, pointing to the monitor. "See for yourself." Braeden came closer to his shipmate's screen and bent down to take a look.

In the lounge, Captain Emil Grant leaned back in his chair, groaned, and threw down his cards. Across from him Duncan Anderson, Chief of Engineering, crowed with delight and scooped up the money from the center of the table.

"Mine again, eh Cap'n?" The cash joined his cache. It was obvious who was winning; the Captain's financial reservoir was considerably depleted and his expression was getting downright grim. "Another?"

"Might as well," he growled. "Your deal, you sleazebag with the luck of an Irishman." Anderson gathered up the cards and started shuffling them. Grant checked his watch and noted he had three hours before he had to make his next token appearance on the bridge. Good. Lots of time to turn things around.

"Captain to the bridge. Captain Grant to the bridge." Braeden's voice, sounding excited and confused, came from the loudspeakers. Grant swore under his breath and got up.

"Grriyll got a hangnail? Or hang sucker or whatever the hell it is she gets?" inquired Anderson.

"Probably. Don't move a muscle." Grant started for the bar then turned back to his Engineer. "And put those cards on the table and keep your sneaky hands off them till I get back," he admonished. Anderson did as he was told, an artfully played hurt expression on his face.

Grant reached the bar and motioned for the bartender to bring him the phone. When it was produced he touched the activator.

"Grant here. What's up?"

"There's a Class IV freighter outside, Captain. Just popped out of hyperspace and heading..."

Grant cut Braeden off. "What are you talking about?"

"We're not sure, sir, but it checks out as that, and she's not showing a beacon."

"Well use the computer then!" What is this, a nursery? Did he have to do all their thinking for them?

"We are, sir. Stand by..." Captain Grant tapped his toe impatiently on the brass foot rail running the length of the bar. Across from him, through the ubiquitous haze that pervades all watering holes, the bartender mixed a drink, eyeing the Captain's worried expression with curiosity...

Grant, like Grriyll and Braeden, found it unusual that a Class IV freighter could be outside. They were designed for intra-system heavy shipping and were therefore incapable of hyperspace Jumps. Even if one had been refitted, though, what in hell was it doing out here in the middle of nowhere? Unless, of course...

Outside, a panel opened in the big freighter's hull and a small parabolic dish slid out until it protruded from the ship's side. The antenna swung to face the liner stopping when it was pointed precisely at the hull outside the bridge. A single blast of bright blue horror leapt from the innocent-looking dish and opened a perfectly round, perfectly lethal hole in the QUEEN VICTORIA'S hull. The two duty officers, who had had no chance to react, were blown into space almost instantly by the rush of escaping atmosphere. An airtight bulkhead slammed into place over the main entrance to the bridge, sealing it from the remainder of the ship until repairs could be made and the room re-pressurized.

As the air trickled into space, emergency circuits automatically took over the load abandoned by the wiring that had been blasted. Farther aft, in passenger and crew territory, the power flickered for a second, then steadied. In Engineering, a technician noticed a few unusual readings and went to check them out.

The intruder turned its gun aft, to the QUEEN VICTORIA's main airlock and, with another blast, tore a circle about three meters in diameter into the outer door. Bits of ruptured hull floated gently away into space as another blast took care of the inner door.

Four bodies, accompanied by assorted tools and spacesuits, squeezed through the hole as the pressure left the liner's foyer. Several automatic airtight doors rammed into place at the inside entrances to the foyer, sealing the body of the ship from the vacuum at both ends.

On the freighter, a huge cargo lock yawned even as the liner was breached, and before it was completely open a horde of armed, black space-suited figures poured out and maneuvered on thruster packs to the liner.

They deployed into a loose sphere surrounding the ship, thirty meters out, covering it with their weapons. One of them went to the emergency airlock, opened the outer door, and gave a hand signal for a second group, split off from the first, to follow him inside. If there had been a casual observer, the entire operation would have looked carefully choreographed, as indeed it was.

Captain Grant ran from the lounge, pounding through corridors and up the fourteen decks to the Bridge, only to find the entrance barred by the airtight door. He stopped, puffing heavily, and swore, then rammed the butt of his hand into the intercom on the port side bulkhead.

"All hands! This is the Captain. We're under attack! Security teams arm yourselves and prepare to repel boarders. Security plan Alpha. Protect our passengers. They must not be harmed. Out." He spun around and headed back down to meet the security team that would take up a position inside the emergency airlock. On his way, passing through Officers' Country, he paused long enough to run to his cabin and collect his sidearm.

Outside the emergency airlock a long tube was being fitted to the QUEEN VICTORIA. It extended across the space between ships, linking the airlocks at both ends. While that was being done, three figures went to the bridge and expanded the hole that had been blasted in the hull, then went inside. One, with well-practiced speed, patched himself into the intraship monitoring system and called up a status report. A bank of screens lit, showing the bedlam inside the liner. Security teams could be seen scrambling to reach their stations, including one on its way to the main airlock. It reached the door sealing it off and then, realizing the way was blocked, stopped confusedly. Smiling, the intruder watched the team's leader go to the intercom and mash its activating button into the bulkhead.

"Security One to Engineering," said a voice. "We're cut off from the main lock. Can you reach it from your side?" Behind him the team fidgeted uncertainly.

"No way," came the reply. "We've tried. We're all trapped down here."

"Damn. Captain Grant..."

"I heard," said the Captain over the intercom. "Stay where you are. If they've got any size of force they're going to have to come through the main lock." The security teams deployed to cover all the routes leading from the evacuated foyer.

On the Bridge, the space-suited figure touched a series of spots on the panel. With a great whoosh, air started rushing from the areas in which the security teams were huddled. A few screamed at the sound, turning and bolting back in the direction they'd come, trying to make it through the next set of airtight bulkheads before they rammed into place farther down the corridor. Some made it; most didn't. One, who'd been lagging behind the others, was crushed as the panel rammed home on top of him. Air leaked around his body as the rest of the team, in panic, tried to pry the bulkhead back up.

It didn't work, and all they succeeded in doing was evacuating the next compartment, causing it to seal off, trapping the pair who'd already managed to escape. They went down, eyes bugging as they learned they couldn't breathe vacuum.

Then, communications silence between the two ships was broken. "Accomplished," was all that was said from the QUEEN VICTORIA's bridge. The figure wreaking remote controlled havoc made a quick count of surviving, and still operative, security team members. He changed frequencies on his radio and said "Six near emergency lock, five with the passengers in the lounge. Move to Stage Two."

The tube joining the ships stiffened as atmosphere flooded through it and at a signal the black figures in the QUEEN VICTORIA's emergency lock removed their helmets. Two were human, the other a Goth, close enough to human for the task. Armored and armed reinforcements from the freighter began erupting into the lock through the tube, and the leader opened the lock's inner door. He ducked as a bolt of energy zipped close by his head.

The fire was returned and in seconds the area was a mass of sizzling energy beams.

In the lounge, the Honorable Representative of Peace from the planet Bolingnar stood up and rattled his pincers in anger. He pointed an accusing appendage. "This is your doing!" he roared. "It has the stench of a dirty Ramallese trick. First you offer peace and invite Federation, then when our backs are turned you do this!" He spat, the saliva hissing angrily on the deck. His entourage growled in agreement behind him.

The Ambassador from Ramallah returned the compliment. "Ha!" it sneered. "As if the Bolingnarian slime is without sin, eh? More likely it is you who arranged this little ambush and are trying to put the blame onto my peace loving people." It shook itself in the classic Ramallese gesture of disgust. "We shall see who is the wronged party here soon enough." It sat down, thereby dismissing the argument as not worthy of continuation, and put its vaporpipe back into its mouth. Its assistants bubbled in defiance of the Bolingnarian outburst.

The Honorable Representative of Peace took a step toward the Ramallan Ambassador, raising a pincer in a movement that was unmistakably unfriendly. A ship's officer stepped between them.

"That's enough, Your Excellencies!" He motioned the Bolingnarian back to his seat. "We must have co-operation! Please!" It wasn't the first time he'd said words to that effect on the voyage, to the same people. The Representative of Peace sat down angrily and stared at the Ramallans, a look that would have curdled blood if the Ramallans had possessed such fluid.

"Keep your heads down!" yelled Grant. He wanted to tell them to take cover, but in the bare passageway there was little point. The only cover was smoke, and it would hardly stop a blaster. Beams met and sizzled as the antagonists tried forcing their collective wills on each other. Four of the liner's crew lay on the deck, unmoving. Only one invader was down.

A puff of smoke appeared on the bulkhead next to the Captain's left ear. He swore and let loose a volley of shots in the direction of the airlock and another enemy lay still.

Then Grant whirled around, crying out and clutching at his thigh. His handgun clattered to the deck. He reached down for it as another beam tore into him. Then another. He went down.

Slowly, inevitably, the attackers pushed the security forces down the passageway, back in the direction from which they had come. By the time they reached the next airtight bulkhead the defenders were dead.

They were turning tables over onto their sides in the lounge, jury-rigging fortifications. Armed crewmembers crouched behind them, waiting.

The Ambassadors had refused to move, ignoring the hullabaloo around them and glaring at each other suspiciously. The Ramallan ordered another drink and a steward ran nervously over to the bar, keeping his head down. The lighting flickered again.

"Here they come!" Clanging, hissing, and snapping could be heard in the distance, getting ever closer. Then the enemy was around the last corner, and in clear view of the lounge.

Three co-coordinated bolts from the defenders brought down the first one. The rest shot back and black, burned circles began appearing on the tabletop/bunkers. One of them started glowing and a few seconds later burst into flames.

In panic, three crewmen arose from behind the table. They were cut down immediately. Another invader dropped at the hands of the crew. The next tripped over the body and fell. The energy beams crisscrossing through the smoke gave the room a soft, eerie glow like a viddy shot on location in Hell. Other fires broke out, adding their own smoke to the already billowing clouds. It was getting hard to see, let alone breathe.

Then it was over. The newcomers spilled into the lounge and a tall, sandy-haired man, obviously the leader, separated from the rest. He waved his arm to clear away some of the smoke. He surveyed the situation.

"Put those fires out," he barked. A couple of his henchmen went behind the bar and returned with extinguishers. They sprayed them on the fires, which died with angry hissing and plenty of steam. When the ventilation system had done its work he pointed to the ambassadors, who were sitting haughtily on the other side of the room, pretending nothing unusual was going on.

"Bring them."

"You will do nothing of the sort, scum," shouted the Honorable Representative of Peace. "I do not care what you were told by those..." he sniffed in disgust, turning his head toward his counterpart,

"...Ramallans. I will not go anywhere."

"Your little world has outdone itself this time, Bolingnarian bandit," accused the other Ambassador. "Hiring mercenaries to do your dirty work now, eh?" It turned to the men. "Do your worst if that's what you've been paid for..." He wiggled a feeler at them, "...but mark my words. Your people and the Bolingnarian bog dwellers will pay dearly for this outrage! My people have a long reach, and an even longer memory."

"Shut up," growled the leader, turning away. "Shut them both up."

It was done without trouble, with a single stun bomb. Still, one of the invaders was hurt when the Bolingnarian's First Assistant raked him with his pincers and grabbed him by the neck in a final, futile attempt at resistance. The human went limp in the creature's grasp and hung there until the gas took effect and its grip loosened. They both collapsed onto the deck in a messy heap.

"Weakling fools!" cried the head Bolingnarian. "You need gas to overcome peaceful civilians?" He spat on the deck then, as his support appendages slid out from under him, gurgled unpleasantly as he joined his counterpart on the deck.

"Let's go," ordered the sandy haired man. Antigravs were attached to the ambassadors' bodies and their limp forms were taken through the passageways to the emergency airlock and across to the freighter. The Bolingnaria and Ramallans were dumped unceremoniously, together, in a storage compartment that had been allocated for the purpose.

The last of the soldiers returned and the tube linking the ships was withdrawn. Shortly afterward, the freighter's drive was activated and the ship pulled away, finally disappearing into hyperspace.

The QUEEN VICTORIA drifted on helplessly.

# VACATED VACATION -- Chapter 2

"I'll put three thousand on twenty three green, second level." A lovely, porcelain-colored female hand that belonged to the soft contralto voice took the chips from a pile in front of her and slid them into the betting bin. The croupier beeped once and said "Three thousand on two-three green, level two," and picked up the bin. It chugged and whirred its way over to the appropriate spot, whereupon it gently placed the lady's bet. "Set."

The robot looked up and down the table to ensure all bets were placed, then touched the sensispot on the game sphere. It started spinning, unsupported in the air, in what was by law, a random manner. The concentric spheres inside spun in different directions until, finally, the outer shell stopped. The croupier opened a tiny door in it and tossed in a small metal ball, then closed the shell, which resumed spinning. All eyes turned to the monitor suspended over the table as the ball gradually worked its way through the spheres toward the innermost one.

The gamblers were a mixed bunch, representing various races of the Co-operative, even the rare crab creature from Kneiapol who leaned over the table, its head encased in the custom helmet that allowed it to breathe what the Kneiapols rather whimsically called, an atmosphere. The other oddity was a semifemale HOQTYNE. Humans, rather unkindly, often called them High Octanes because of their annoying habit of passing rich grade gas at the most inappropriate moments. Other than that, the gamblers ran the biped gamut, from human to birdlike Avitites.

The giant casino was crowded and noisy. It was after midnight, though one couldn't tell that because the exits and windows were deliberately isolated from the gambling areas, ensuring that no signs of life were visible from the gambling hall. No clocks were in evidence.

The Spheres were slowing, from the outer, concentrically, to the middle. With a final "chink" of the metal ball falling into a hole, the game hummed to a stop and the croupier took a quick look, via monitor, at where the ball had landed. "Second level, two-three green," it announced in its metallic twang.

There were cries of disgust in many languages as the croupier hauled in the losses. The porcelain-complexioned lady, who wriggled with delight and squealed "Oh, my goodness, I win again!" was the exception. The croupier delivered her plunder and dumped it in front of her. The woman picked up the chips and poured them carelessly into a case slung over her shoulder, leaving enough on the table to be considered a generous tip. The robot droned an absent "Management thanks you" as she turned to leave.

The eyes of the male humans at the table followed the woman as she walked away from the game. Her hair was black as the interstellar night, and the side of her that could be seen disappearing from the table displayed cascades of it reaching almost to the roundness of an all-too-human behind. As if sensing what the men were thinking, the lady paused as she passed a huge mirror that ran from the floor to the high ceiling. She smiled and blew herself a quick kiss.

The woman sauntered over to one of the old fashioned slot machines that were lined up in rows near a wall, the electronic "One armed bandits" that had been swallowing suckers' silver for centuries, and dropped a stollar into its slot. She slouched back a step, resting with one foot planted behind the other, and a little sideways, as she waited for the displays to stop moving. They finally did, showing three galaxies, and a cascade of coinage clattered into the bin. She scooped the booty into her case, grinning broadly, and straightened up to leave.

She took the skyway to the lobby of the adjoining hotel and went to the desk, behind which a clerk was leaning on his knuckles, staring into space with a bored expression. "Eighteen forty three, please," she said after clearing her throat to get his attention. The clerk typed the number into the terminal as she touched her thumb to the counter's sensispot.

"No messages," he said.

"Thanks." She took the lift tube to her floor and went down the long, wide hallway with its cheap murals depicting the deserts of old Earth's Nevada, after which Gault's gambling Mecca had been patterned and named. She stopped at 1843, touched her thumb to the sensispot on the door and, when it slid open, went into her suite. The door closed behind her. She paused and lit the "Do Not Disturb" sign before moving into the room.

"How's it goin'?" she asked the secretary as she passed it on her way to the bedroom. The machine made a whirring noise as it ran through its memory, then beeped once and reported everything was fine. In a moment, the woman, having changed into a loose-fitting robe, came back into the living room. She plopped down onto the sofa.

"Glenfiddich neat, please." The bar turned on and poured the drink, which the valet wheeled over to her. She took the glass from the machine, swallowed a deep slug of the liquor, and set the glass on the coffee table. "Video, please." A section of wall slid sideways, revealing a large screen that lit up with the menu of available programming. She made her selection with the remote control that was laying on the coffee table and the display changed to a mildly erotic threedee.

"Another scotch, please." She was beginning to feel lightheaded, something she couldn't often afford, but could tonight. The Gandibar affair had really put her through the wringer, but she wouldn't have to go through that any more. Auntie's reaction to her resignation had been more unpleasant than she'd expected, but what the hell. It was over.

. The crackling of the empty video signal woke her. She turned off the unit, got up, and headed unsteadily for the bedroom, bouncing off a wall only once. In the back of her mind she realized she probably should have quit about three Glenfiddichs earlier, but it was her vacation. She curled up in the soft decadence of the sleeper, shushed out the lights, and within seconds was snoring loudly and quite unmusically.

There was an insistent clanging inside her head, a loud and annoying ringing that refused to stop. It curled in and around her consciousness like a slithering viper, vying for attention with her haunted dreams of missions past, of worlds and people in conflict, of death and destruction. The dreams would vary in setting and intensity, but the damn ringing kept up until she could stand it no longer and fought her way back through the horror to the edge of reality. She sat up in bed, drenched in a cold sweat.

The doorbell was howling like a banshee, as if whoever was responsible for the hubbub had been there for a while and was getting awfully impatient.

"Damn. Oh, God," she muttered and lay down again, covering her head with the pillow. It did nothing to eliminate the insistent ringing, though, let alone assuage the massively oversized head she was wearing. Finally, she swore and sat up again, reaching for the robe she'd left on a chair beside the bed. She pulled it on and got up, dragging herself into the living room and over to the door.

"Whaddya want?" she demanded into the screener. It had to be a mistake. No one was supposed to know where she was staying, or when, or as whom. But there was always Murphy's Law...

"Bonnie Day?" came a voice from the hallway, slightly metallic-sounding through the screener. Double damn! But she wasn't about to go down that easily.

"You've got the wrong guy. Go away."

"Lieutenant Bonnie Day, 19th Irregulars? We know it's you, Miz Day." There was a pause while the speaker let the fact sink in. "We have orders to speak with you. Hallelujah, sister."

Day sighed. "Great," she muttered, "Just ducky." They had her name and rank correct, but what really bugged her was the password.

It told her they'd stay there, leaning on the bell until either Hell froze over or she opened up, whichever came first. Bidding a mental farewell to her anonymity and her vacation, she swallowed once and gave in to the inevitable. She touched the sensispot and allowed the door to open.

Three large, extremely male examples of the Space Marines stood in the hallway. They were spit and polish men all, tall, with faces so cleanly scrubbed and shaven she could have put on her makeup by her reflection off their chins, if it didn't blind her first. The peculiar Marine sheen did nothing to help her hung-over eyes and she lowered them, squinting, while the most massive of the Marines gave her the once over.

"Whaddya want?" she growled. So they knew who she was, big deal. She just wanted to sleep or, better still, die. Just for a while.

"Lieutenant you have orders to report to the Chief of Operations, Mobile Intelligence Command. We're your escort."

Figured. "I don't work there any more. Beat it."

"I don't know about that, Miz, but we have orders."

"Too bad. I'm sleeping."

"You don't appear to be sleeping any more, Miz. Sorry, these orders say immediately." He smiled wolfishly. "You got time to freshen and get dressed, though. You know?"

"Thanks a bundle." She opened the door wide and headed back to the bedroom, motioning the Marines inside. "Make yourselves at home, boys. I'll be ready in an hour."

It actually took an hour and forty five minutes but when she was finished she looked, and almost felt, ready to face the universe again. Fortunately, the suite's biffy was well equipped to handle the stresses of the high roller gambling lifestyle. For insurance, Day took a precautionary double dose of their most powerful analgesic.

She'd dressed in a loose fitting, professional-looking suit that was designed to conceal many of the toys with which she'd chosen to arm herself. After a quick reconnaissance in the mirror to ensure nothing showed that she didn't want showing, she returned to the living room. The Marines tried their best not to look at her too appreciatively, but didn't manage it very well. Day didn't mind. Sometimes looks could work to one's advantage. Besides, while they'd had been looking her up and down she'd been doing the same to them and had decided that, if she had to, she could take them. They were only Marines. Which reminded her. She'd been damn sloppy in her hung-over haze. "Lemme see your ID," she ordered gruffly, mentally kicking herself for not having demanded to see their chips before she'd let them in. The identification was produced without comment and looked fine, which made her breathe easier, though it didn't actually prove anything. Space Service identification was the devil to forge and she was confident she could spot a fake at forty paces. Well, twenty.

"Okay, let's go. Bring my bags." They went down the lift tube and out the hotel's main entrance. Day blinked in the oppressively glaring sunlight and looked around. It was winter on Gault, so there was only a mild cloud cover marring the blazing yellow of the sky, allowing the planet's primary to beat down unmercifully on the heads of creatures foolish enough to be outside without protection. The air was bone dry, still as death, and stiflingly hot. Day cringed and shielded her eyes with her hand, wishing the medications would hurry up and kick in.

She was led to the Northbound slidewalk and they got on. The low, thrumming whine of its mechanism did little to help Day's head and she braced herself for what would be an unpleasant half hour's trip to the spaceport, which was surely where they were heading. Vehicles had been banned within New Las Vegas' city limits ever since the infamous riots of '43, when irate tourists had revolted against crooked taxi drivers. Taxis, buses or whatever, were only allowed at the spaceport, and people wanting to visit Gault's other Meccas had to go there to hire transport.

Long before they reached the port the analgesics took effect and Day felt in possession of her faculties once again. She took stock of the situation and decided that, since she had no intention of reporting as ordered and there weren't enough people on the slidewalks to let her blend in with a crush of humanity, if she made a break for it, the best place would be in the always-crowded terminal. She relaxed and tried to enjoy the ride, while planning her escape. If they were taking her offworld, back to Endikar Base, the hairy apes would have to take her through the terminal to a ship. That seemed logical, since the Club hadn't opened its Gault branch yet. She decided that must be what they were planning, so there should be plenty of opportunity at the Port for her to get away.

That meant it was time to start winning them over, to make them think she had accepted her fate. "So where we heading?" she asked pleasantly.

The massive Marine who'd chosen to be spokesman looked at her blandly. "Dunno, Miz. We're just supposed to get you to the 'Port in one piece and see you get on your transport. They don't tell us nothin'." He shrugged and tried to smile, but it didn't suit his face. "Sorry."

She smiled back, one of her patented ones. "Don't worry about it."

The smallest of the three piped up "You in some kinda trouble, Miz?"

She shook her head and gave another Smile. "No. Just a little overdue, if anything." Marines were pieces of cake. Beefcake.

"Well I hope they go easy on you," the short one continued. "You're an awfully pretty lady to get in trouble." She gave an outwardly friendly, inwardly incredulous, smile at the man's illogical statement.

The seemingly endless line of gaudy casinos, hotels, and other money traps that lined the slidewalk was finally thinning and the moving way brought them to a junction. They changed over to the Port-bound slidewalk and in a few minutes the huge terminal came into view ahead of them. For Gault, it was a tasteful complex, crammed to bursting with people and vehicles of all descriptions. It was long overdue for renovation, but the Gault council had been too busy counting and pocketing money to bother with spending any. Traffic buzzed around overhead like a swarm of angry hornets, their noise added to the already cacophonous atmosphere, making Day grateful her hangover was finally gone.

The slidewalk was becoming progressively more crowded as they neared the spaceport but Day, flanked as she was by the burly blaster bait, had yet to find that sudden, Golden Opportunity, that would allow her to make her break. They passed through the automatic doors, back into the blessed relief of the air conditioning, and in moments were on the "Local Traffic" side of the terminal.

The noise was incredible. Gambling machines paid off with loud "chings!" and the accompanying rattle of stollars dropping into hoppers, while horribly intrusive music blared from the speakers in a cacophony designed to welcome, or bid an early return to, the millions of tourists who visited the planet each year. It was a well orchestrated party atmosphere.

Day and her escort got off at an open area and headed toward a sign marked "RESTRICTED AREA." Day looked around, sizing up the situation. Beyond the sign there was no crowd, no diversions, no escape. She decided it was now or never.

"Listen," she said, prodding the big Marine with her elbow, "I gotta pee. I'll be right back." She headed for the ladies room before he could protest and, once inside, chose a stall.

A couple of rapid shrugs had her suit off, revealing her personal arsenal. She was packing projectile and beam launching weapons, along with some that were smaller and much more subtle. Right then it was subtlety that was called for, and what she wanted was inside a hidden compartment in her purse. She took out a bottle and some makeup, followed by a small mirror. She got busy then, with a flush, the evidence of her chicanery disappeared.

The Marines leaned against the wall outside the rest room, eyes judging each passing female, some of whom were in states of Gault attire that gave plenty to judge. They hardly gave the bag lady a glance as she limped out of the washroom, just enough of a look to convince them they didn't want to see any more.

Day was almost to the taxi stand outside before the alarm went off and the doors slammed shut behind her. Uniformed security guards swarmed out of the terminal, brandishing their weapons, while the public address system brayed for everyone to stand still and get ready to be inspected. She ignored the kerfuffle, opened the door of the nearest taxi, and slid into the back seat. "Nouveau Taheau, please."

The driver, an ugly beast from the dregs of the Degenerais, turned to face her. "Are you kidding, lady?" he said with a surly sneer. He took in her shabby attire and bedraggled looks. "Whattya think I am? A charity?" His expression was sullen, with traces of boredom peeking around the edges. It changed to one of amazement, though, when he saw the blaster Day had pointing at him. Amazement and fear.

"You'll take off now like I said," she hissed, reaching over the seat back and prodding him with the weapon. He shrugged what passed for shoulders and started up the machine. It leapt into the sky. Day noticed in passing that he hadn't forgotten to start the meter.

It didn't take long for the sound of pursuing sirens to be heard over the whining of the cab's engines. Day swiveled around to look out the rear window; they were about three klicks up and climbing, but the cab wasn't any match for their pursuers.

"Can't you go any faster?" she asked.

"No lady this is all she's got." He sniffed mightily and wiped his noses with the back of his hand. Then a transparent panel slammed shut between them and Day heard a roar as a thick, blue haze flooded into the passenger compartment.

Dozegas!

Day lifted her blaster and rayed open a hole in the barrier between her and the driver. The beam continued through the driver and the windshield and the suddenly uncontrolled cab began to fall, rocking and twisting sickeningly. Day was thrown from side to side as it spun crazily toward the ground. She tried to grab the door control, but was slammed to the other side of the cab instead. She reached for the control on that side and missed again. Her head was slammed into the sidelight, dazing her. Below, the ground twisted and turned nauseatingly, getting closer with each rotation of the cab. Day braced her back against the seat and her feet against the partition, aimed her blaster at the side window, and fired.

# AUNTIE'S ESTABLISHMENT -- Chapter 3

The taxi hit hard and exploded, sending a black cloud rising above the dirty plain of Eastern Gault. The cab burned fiercely for a few moments then, when the combustibles had been combusted, the fire died out, leaving a smoldering mass of barbecued, unrecognizable junk.

Three kilometers south, Bonnie Day hit hard and rolled with the impact. She shook her head, got to her feet, brushed herself off, and began folding her mini-chute. She stuffed it back into the pouch under her clothes and looked toward the horizon, where smoke still rose thickly.

She smiled and mentally patted herself on the back. A pretty good getaway, that. Not perfect, but it had worked out okay. With luck, and the typically thorough detective work for which the Gault Police were famous, they'd think she was dead. Auntie and the Club, too. Good. Peace and quiet was what she wanted, though she should have known better than to look for it in New Las Vegas.

Day glanced up at the sun to get her bearings, squinting in the brightness. She did a few calculations, chose a direction, and started walking.

It only took a few kilometers for her to become dead tired and red-hot. She wiped the sweat from her face and pushed her hair back out of her eyes. New Las Vegas was farther than she had thought, but her choices in the matter were limited: press on or roast. There was no shelter.

Fire.

Blinding light.

Burning heat. The flames scorched the inside of Day's head, entering through her eyes, her ears, boring its way right through the top of her skull. She felt as if her brain were about to start boiling at any minute. She put her hands over her head, ineffectively, trying to shelter herself from the death raining down on her. In the back of her mind she wondered how long she'd been out there in the sun, risking a roasting.

Day lifted her head from the melting sand and spat out a mouthful of the grit. Gently, carefully, she looked around. Just desert. Her just desserts? She smiled grimly, amazed that she could still joke. She was dead tired. Sleep was the order of the day, a long rest to just relax and recharge her dehydrated body until the desert evening embraced her and it was cool enough to travel. She lay her head back on the sand and closed her eyes.

No! She'd end up well done, an evening buffet for the birds that were already spiraling expectantly above her. Summoning all her remaining strength, Day managed to pull herself to her feet and staggered on a few paces. God, she needed a drink! Even water.

Especially water. Beautiful, cool water.

And cool, shady palms, their fronds waving gently in the summer breeze...

The dirt in her mouth made Day realize she'd stumbled and fallen again. As she lifted her head from the ground, she noticed a stain on the sand below her and her heart fell. Had one of those flying jackals already started pecking at her? Then she realized she'd merely sweated off the makeup she'd used to camouflage her appearance from the Marines. She thought absently that she must look like something out of a cheap horror show and, if it weren't that she was so damn tired, so damn thirsty, she would have been mildly entertained by the mental picture it gave. Slowly, she hauled herself back to her feet, groaning, and stumbled onward.

Was that a mirage? She'd fallen again, but this time as she'd gone down she thought she'd seen a dark spot on the desert ahead, in a little, otherwise bleak rock outcropping. She squinted toward the apparition, through the watery-looking haze rising off the desert in front of her. It sure looked like a cave, a dark pool of cool in the middle of the burning agony. She rose to her knees, then slowly stood, swaying crazily like a scarecrow in a strong breeze. She staggered forward.

And literally fell into the shadows where she was immediately enveloped by their blessed coolness. Gasping at the unheated air gratefully, she collapsed onto the hard, rocky, downwardly sloping floor of the cave and rolled into the blessed darkness.

Day lay there, unmoving, for what must have been hours, then opened her eyes, rolled over, and sat up. Her eyes opened more widely as the memory of her ordeal washed over her. Then she smiled.

Day took inventory of her situation. She was obviously alive, and the cave in front of her extended into darkness of indeterminate depth. After a few minutes, she decided that, wherever it led, it would be a hell of a lot more comfortable than the desert she'd left outside. She'd wait until dark and then continue on to New Las Vegas, but in the meantime...

She got up, brushed herself off, and went exploring.

Less than a hundred meters down the tunnel Day thought she could see a glimmer ahead. A couple of bends in the tunnel later she knew there was definitely a light farther down the tunnel. It was too steady to be a fire; in fact it looked like standard indoor lighting. She slowed down and carefully rounded another corner, which brought the light very close. It appeared to be just over a medium high rock wall ahead. She crouched low and sneaked forward until she was only separated from the light by the wall, then rose up on her heels and sneaked a peek at what was beyond.

Day groaned and stood up. The light was coming from a ceiling fixture in a well-lit reception area that, except for it being in a cave, could have been from any office on any civilized planet. Well, not just any office, for the man sitting at the plush desk in front of the broad plastique door was well known to her. And he was staring right at her, smiling like the cat who ate the canary.

"Hello, Supra 9!" the man said, the merry glint in his eyes getting merrier. "Fancy meeting you out here!" Day swore in a most unladylike manner and moved out into the room. "Save," the man said in the direction of the computer monitor on the desk as he got up and came around to meet her, cluck clucking over her sun baked appearance. He was middle aged, though Day had always thought he carried it well for an old fart. Slightly shorter than she, he had a reasonable build, a thick mane of crimson hair, and a full and matching red beard. He looked exactly as he always had, right down to the silly ascot around his rotten neck. "Tut, tut, Bonnie," he said, looking her up and down, "Don't you know enough to come in out of the hot?"

"How you keeping, Butt Breath?" Bonnie managed to reply with as much ice as possible in her voice.

"Just great, hon. It's good to see you." The man, Day knew, held a genuine fondness for her. It was generally reciprocated, but at this point in time she wasn't inclined to greet this intrusion from her former life too kindly.

"Not long enough. So they've opened the Gault branch, eh?"

"Not quite. We're supervising the final touches. You knew we were opening one, didn't you?"

Day nodded. "I suggested it, but I didn't think it would be ready this soon."

"Well it's close enough."

"I suppose Auntie's here?"

"Of course."

"I was hoping she'd made me an unperson. You know, erase the kilobytes of memory that said I ever existed."

"Not likely, Supra 9." Day took stock of the stone walled room. It was as plain as a cave could be except that, besides the tunnel through which she'd entered the place, there were two plastique doors built into the living rock walls. The richly finished one set into the wall behind the reception desk undoubtedly led to Auntie's office, while the plain one in the side wall would open onto the rest of the

Clubhouse.

Day looked back at the man she had so affectionately called "Butt Breath." His name was Bert Brecht, but Bonnie had always addressed him in her somewhat more casual manner. "Mister Breath" didn't seem to mind, at least he'd never said anything to Day.

She brought herself back to her present situation, shaking her head to clear it. "What did you say?" she said. It was so much more intelligent-sounding than her initial answer, which would have been "Huh?"

"I said it's not very likely that Auntie would clear your name from memory." Day sat on the corner of Brecht's desk, since they hadn't seen fit to bring along a chair for anyone in the waiting room.

Brecht looked Day over. He'd never seen her look worse, though he'd never been in the field to witness the banging up she'd taken sometimes. He'd read the reports, though, and knew that, Bonnie Day being who she was, she'd be back to normal after a good bath and a couple of stiff scotches.

"I'm glad you're all right, Bonnie. And I'm sure Auntie will be pleased to see you."

"Who gives a rat's...."

"Now, now," he interrupted quickly. He motioned behind him, to the closed door. "You two have some catching up to do and you can't leave here without at least saying hello."

"Try me."

Brecht tut tutted and shook his head. "Just go talk to her. What harm can that do?"

"You'd be surprised." Day hopped down from the desk corner anyway, turned on her heel, and went toward the door behind Brecht. It "shusshed" open when she got near. Despite herself, Day's skin began to tingle in anticipation, the way it always had when she was about to meet Auntie, and she unconsciously reached her hand to her matted hair in a vain attempt to make it a little more presentable.

"Come in, Supra 9," ordered a booming, powerful and too-familiar voice. "We should talk." At the sound, Day got an annoyed look on her face, remembering all the reasons she'd vowed never to see Auntie again. But she crossed the threshold and went into the room.

It was very dark, as always, with the inevitable pool of light from an overhead fixture lapping at the big desk at the opposite end of the room. Sitting in the darkness behind the desk, Day knew, was Auntie. She smiled grimly at the name. Who or what Auntie was Day couldn't say, and she'd been guessing for what already seemed a lifetime. Day'd never been able to make out any of Auntie's features, if indeed she had any worth remembering; Auntie had always preferred to remain a shadowy enigma.

"Sit down, Supra 9," Auntie ordered and Day walked over to and sat in the big, overstuffed visitor's chair across the marble desk from where Auntie waited. Thoughtfully, and within easy reach of Day's chair, a pitcher of water and one large glass had been left. Despite her tiredness, Day sat straight and tall, and stared into the puddle of dark across from her, at where her ex-boss, "Club President," hid.

"Mind if I have a drink?"

There was a soft gurgle from the shadow. "Go ahead. You must be a trifle thirsty." Day poured a glassful and downed it quickly, then had another, and another. She poured a fourth and took a long draw, then put the glass back onto the desk and put on her best exasperated look.

"What's the idea of sending those Marine maroons to haul me in?" she said. "You have no right to interfere with my life!"

There was a slight chuckle from the darkness. "No right, you say. Is that how you express your gratitude for being saved from a most uncomfortable afternoon in the garden spot of this ridiculous planet?"

"*You* saved *me*? I seem to have found your hidey hole all by myself."

"And a lucky break it was, wasn't it?" Again, the slight chuckle, then: "But I don't understand your anger, Supra 9. I didn't send anyone to find you. I hadn't quite gotten around to it yet. Have you been getting into trouble again?"

"Like hell. I left trouble behind when I tore up my membership card."

"Perhaps someone carries a grudge?"

That had always been a possibility, something about which she'd thought long and hard before resigning, but it hadn't changed her mind to get out of the troubleshooting business and into a different line of work.

Troubleshooting. The job description was a bad joke, just like the Club. She'd seen more than enough trouble and more than enough shooting. That's why she'd quit: she'd reached her threshold.

"Maybe," she said. "I'd hoped I'd scraped all that off my shoes."

"I seem to remember us going over this at length when you tendered your resignation. I also seem to remember telling you that the Club carries with it a lifetime membership. You chose to ignore that."

"Yeah, well, hindsight's great, isn't it?" Not her snappiest comeback, but it was true nonetheless. "You have any idea who might want to grab me?"

"You mean besides the obvious gaggle of people?"

Day frowned, preferring not to try counting the names on that particular list; it was a long one. "Of course. Do you have anyone new in mind, since I've been out?"

Was that a bit of a sniff from the darkness? "Unfortunately, no," said Auntie. "In fact, we've run into a bit of trouble in that regard ourselves."

Day swallowed. For Auntie to admit a bit of trouble meant all hell was breaking loose. "Trouble. That's your business isn't it?"

"Unfortunately, the Club still fulfills a needed function. And may I suggest it's time for you to return?"

"Forget it." Day stood up, taking her glass of water with her. "Just because someone sent some fake Marines after me doesn't mean I'm going to forget my life, my plans. I'll just have to keep my eyes more open."

"For the rest of your natural life..."

"If necessary. I've made my bed."

"Hear me out, Supra 9," said Auntie, quickly. "There's more than you know, and it may affect you and your plans directly."

"I don't care," Day said. But she returned to the chair.

"Thank you for giving me the courtesy."

Day mumbled something under her breath.

"Perhaps later," Auntie replied softly. "Now, if I may continue, this attempt on you fits a pattern we've seen far too much of lately."

"What do you mean?"

"I mean, Bonnie, that you are the only Supra remaining." Auntie stopped to let the significance of the bombshell sink in. Day sat back in her chair and knitted her fingers together, her forehead wrinkling in thought.

"I don't suppose they've all quit," she said, finally, lamely.

Auntie sighed. "Of course not, Supra 9. They're dead. All of them. Killed individually."

Day whistled. "How?"

"Various methods. I can give you a file. Someone wants the Club eliminated and is very close to succeeding. That's why we're here, where we don't have an official presence yet."

"Hiding, eh?" It made sense. If someone knew enough to get at the other fifteen Supras, then someone had inside information about the Club, and was well organized and financed. Moving the operation to the newest Clubhouse, one that few would know of, could buy Auntie and the organization some time. "Why is someone doing this?"

"Besides the obvious reasons of hate and revenge, I can't think why. I was hoping you could."

"I dunno, you've given me such extensive background material," Day said sarcastically. "Do you have any clues?"

"No. Each Supra's death was violent, but appeared unrelated. I would think if it was someone we've dealt with in the past they would want to leave some sort of calling card, so we'd know who'd defeated us."

"Unless they want to wait until the job's done...with my death. Or yours."

"Perhaps. But think of this, too, Supra 9. While all of you have made innumerable enemies in the past, none of you have made all the same enemies. It doesn't make sense."

"Unless it's a preemptive strike."

"Correct."

"Are you sure the Supras are all dead?"

"No, but I must assume the worst. We've recovered five bodies; the rest have been out of contact an inordinately long time and we've been unable to raise them on the implants."

"Then they're dead."

"That is what we assume."

"Anything big on the go?"

"Not big, at least not yet, but there is something happening that is important for the Co-operative over the long term and it may be related. You know of the Ramallan and Bolingnarian peace initiative?"

"Of course. The bonehead worlds."

"The Co-operative prefers to look on those races as...immature."

"Whatever. What's the story?" Auntie brought Day up to date with the negotiations, how both sides had agreed to meet in a neutral environment the Co-operative was more than happy to provide for them. How the Bolingnaria and Ramallans had allowed delegations to meet aboard a Co-operative-registered liner, and how all contact with the ship had been lost two weeks before.

"And hasn't anyone gone to look?" asked Day.

"Supra 4 was on board the QUEEN VICTORIA, ostensibly as a crewmember. He hasn't been heard from, obviously. Supra 14 was about to leave last week, right after we got word of the, er, loss of contact. He died before he could go."

"You mean that was the last attempt?"

"I've been understandably busy, Supra 9. It's up to you to go."

"Me? Yeah, right. I don't work here, remember?"

Day heard that sigh from the darkness across the desk. "Supra 9. Do we need to get into this again? You're my last agent. You're already being hunted. Do I need to draw you a picture?"

"Get out your handy dandy indelible markers and draw away." If Auntie thought she was going to give up her hard won freedom for a couple of races of ignoramuses, she was crazy. She was sorry to hear about the other agents, but that, after all, was the risk they took in the job every day. Life was tough sometimes.

"Supra 9. Bonnie. This case is exceedingly important to the Co-operative. I'm sure you understand its significance."

"Of course. The government wants the public relations coup of helping bring peace to Bolingnar and Ramallah, then admitting them to the Co-operative and thereby expanding its sphere of influence and its credibility. It was a Co-op sponsored round of negotiations in a Co-op-registered ship. It wants the glory and just as important it wants the brownie points. That still has nothing to do with me."

"Please reconsider. Until I can find and train some new operatives, you're my last hope."

"Well, thanks for the testimonial," she said more casually than she felt. "I'll ask Butt Breath out there for a transcript next time I need to put a resume together." She leaned back in the chair and tried putting her feet on the edge of Auntie's desk, but it was too high. "But as far as your proposal goes, I'm sorry but I'm otherwise occupied."

Auntie growled, a sound Day had never heard emanate from her former boss before. "Don't make me force you, Supra 9."

"You and who else?"

"I'd prefer not having to invoke any special orders. I'd prefer your cooperation be given freely, but you know the means I have at hand to use when necessary. The choice is yours."

Day snorted. She knew well. "Choice? I come back and work for you or you take my balls and go home, right?"

# BACK IN THE SADDLE AGAIN -- Chapter 4

Bert Brecht looked up from his monitor and smiled when the door sighed open and Bonnie Day reappeared. "Save," he told the computer and turned to face her. "Well, I don't see any bruises, not that I could make them out under all that dirt. Everything all right?"

"Stuff it," Day said angrily. Brecht's smile disappeared. "How can you keep working for that machine?"

He shrugged. "Job security and great benefits."

"Always the entrepreneur, eh, Butt Breath?"

"I'm a career civil servant Bonnie, and I don't want my grandchildren going barefoot."

"Government job, huh?" Despite her anger and frustration, she smiled. Brecht had never been anything but supportive and sympathetic to her and, after all, couldn't be blamed for placing his loyalties where they'd do him the most good. "You'll never have to work again. Must be nice."

"Thanks."

"What do you know about what's going on?"

Brecht shrugged. "Not much. None of us do." He glanced in the direction of the doorway through which Day had just exited. "It's really got the old bag spooked. Nothing like this has happened before and she's fit to be tied."

"Should be tied and gagged and spaced."

Brecht smiled. "Don't be too hard on her, Bonnie. It's been a rough couple of months, and though you may not know it, Auntie really cares for all of her Supras. Losing them like this has really had an effect on her."

"Hmmm. What's in the vehicle pool?"

"Not much, I'm afraid. The outpost isn't quite on line yet, and not everything's installed." Brecht pressed a couple of keys and consulted his monitor. "It depends how you want to go. There's a Martin Flying Harness that'll get you over to New Las Vegas pretty quick. You could get a transport there. We're only about five klicks outside the city, you know."

"That figures." A Martin Flying Harness was light and fun and would be perfect for a short hop like that, at least during the cool of the desert night, but it was useless for going off planet. That would leave her with trying to find something suitable from the public renters when she got to New Las Vegas, and that would be a pain in the rear end. It would also leave an obvious trail. Day looked down at her arms; they were turning deep red and would begin to peel before long. Perhaps something air-conditioned, maybe with a nice, synthohide interior. "What else you got? Something for space, and with some toys. You know me."

"How 'bout a new Xannyk? Loaded, naturally."

"Isn't that the way they come?" Day's ears perked up. Xannyks were hot, with creature comforts enough for any creature, as long as it was bipedal. "I'll take it."

Brecht did something at the computer, then smiled conspiratorially. "It's all yours. Have fun. And good luck, Bonnie." He motioned to the other door cut into the rock and his hand went below the desktop to a hidden button. The door swung open, revealing a short tunnel beyond.

"Thanks, Bert." Day gave him a quick peck on the cheek and headed through the opening. The door closed behind her with a muffled thud. Good insulation, she thought.

The tunnel was paneled in what appeared to be real Shemly, but that was about as far as the appointments had gotten. There was no finish on the floor, though from the way the synthcrete was marked up Day could tell it wouldn't be long before the situation was rectified.

A metal door at the other end of the tunnel swung aside as she approached it and on the other side the hallway opened onto a couple of nondescript, unfurnished rooms that could function as offices, bedrooms, or whatever, depending upon how they were eventually furnished. Lavatories were next, followed by a larger conference/recreation room that was also unoccupied. Farther along was yet another, larger door. It opened when Day approached and she entered into the garage beyond. The door slid shut behind her with the muffled thud of a bombproof.

The garage was housed inside a huge, natural cavern with a ceiling that was lost in the shadows above the lighting fixtures' artificial illumination. The walls were about fifty meters apart and at the far side of the garage there was another example of a typical bombproof door - large enough to permit entrance and exit of anything up to a medium sized transport. Day spotted the Xannyk Brecht had promised her, a lovely yacht, and caressed its sleek lines with her eyes before taking in the rest of the inventory. Brecht had been right when he said there wasn't much in the way of transport. Besides the Xannyk, there were three nondescript two-person flyers and, hanging on one wall, the Flying Harness.

"Well, well, if it isn't lovely to see you again, S-S-S-Supra 9!" came a friendly bellow. Day turned to look, a broad smile appearing on her face. Sitting at a workbench, a huge yellow thing with four tentacles and a long tail sat working on some piece of equipment. There were no legs in evidence. The yellow head was split by what would be considered a grin by most humanoids and the creature's gelatinous flesh jiggled and rippled with delight.

"Why you old aspic!" Day shouted, running toward the creature and wrapping her arms around it, carefully, so as not to rupture the outer membrane and cause it to run. "How you been, Jing?"

"Just fine, B-B-B-Bonnie, just fine. Golly gee, it's good to see you again. You've looked b-b-b-better, though." Day let go her hug and stroked Jing gently under its chin-compatible. The creature gurgled appreciatively.

"It's been a rough day, but it's nothing a good soak won't clear up."

"Good! I suppose you've come for t-t-t-transport."

"Yup." She pointed to the gleaming, silver space yacht resting majestically near the door, looking like it wanted nothing better than to leap into space. From the model number on its hull, she could tell the ship was outfitted to its maximum and, knowing Jing, it would also be loaded with all sorts of other interesting options not readily visible nor available from the factory. "The Xannyk."

"Good choice. She's a real b-b-b-beauty," Jing told her. "Wish I could drive it, but I'm not b-b-b-built that way. How'd you get Auntie to let you requisition it? It's her ship. Bet she put up some kind of fuss, eh?"

So that was why Brecht had smiled when he'd authorized Day to take the ship. She smiled at the thought of Auntie having to give up her yacht. Served her right. Let *her* take the Martin! "Where you h-h-h-headed?"

"Gotta date with a cruise ship." Day figured her first order of business would be to poke around the QUEEN VICTORIA and see what she could dig up there. On the way, she'd review the data on the case and the missing agents. "Please download file 'Daylight One' to the Xannyk's computer," she said.

"S-s-s-sure," replied Jing, turning to his computer. "Want me to go over the ship with you?" Jing flowed onto the floor from his stool, his way of standing, and picked up a thick manual.

"That's for the Xannyk?" Jing's head undulated up and down, his version of a nod. "Naw, we'd be here for the rest of my life. Just make sure it's got a good help program and I'll play with it as I go. I've driven Xannyks before." She walked over to the gleaming ship and ran her hand appreciatively down its side.

"I don't b-b-b-blame you for wanting to experiment. Xannyk makes great ships, but their documentation is t-t-t-terrible." Jing stretched out a pseudopod and flowed into it, moving toward Day. "This one's help program is built right in. You just talk to the computer. You'll have fun." The creature reached Bonnie and stretched out an 'arm-compatible,' flowing it around her shoulders.

"Be careful, B-B-B-Bonnie. Bring that ugly hide back. The y-y-y-yacht too."

"Don't worry." Day gave the creature another gentle hug, then they separated. Jing flowed back to his computer and motioned for Day to put her thumb on the pad by the Xannyk's airlock. She did so, and Jing murmured some instructions. The thumb pad under Day's appendage lit for a second as the yacht memorized her unique whorls and changed the security authorization.

"It's all y-y-y-yours now, B-B-B-Bonnie," said Jing. The airlock's outer door glided silently open and Day stepped inside. She turned and waved to Jing, then touched her thumb to the pad by the inner door. It opened.

The airlock opened onto what served as the bridge, though it was more like a living room that doubled as an office and featured an oversized desk facing the large viewscreen. Comfy-looking chairs sat behind the desk, and in the center of the room was a luxurious sofa and coffee table. The big viewscreen looked more like the video wall in her apartment than the typical computer monitor-cum-viewport of most ships.

Day was immediately taken by the ship's workmanship. It was almost decadent, with gilded curlicues and jeweled buttons bringing back memories of designs centuries old. Xannyk had upped the ante since she'd last been in one of their products, probably to compete with the new brands that were vying for a slice of the luxury space yacht pie. Day approved.

"Hello," said the computer in an all-too-human voice as lights began chasing each other across the various monitoring panels. "You're obviously Supra 9. Welcome aboard. May I serve you?" There was a soft whirring noise from somewhere, and Day could feel the soft breath of a breeze as the air-conditioning started.

"Not unless you're a cannibal," Day retorted. "I'd like a status report, please."

"All my systems are ready, Supra 9. I'm very well maintained."

"I can imagine. But don't call me Supra 9. I'm Bonnie."

"Okay, Bonnie, you're the user. May I say it's nice to have you aboard?"

Day liked a computer with personality, but hoped it wouldn't turn out to be one of those that fawned all the time. They wore thin very quickly. "Thanks. Open communication to the hangar, please."

"Jing is in circuit," the machine said as the gelatinous creature appeared on the main screen.

"Thanks. Hi, Jing. Nice tub you've got here," she said appreciatively.

"What d-d-d-did you expect? A NewFord?" Jing gurgled pleasantly at Day.

"Jing, old friend, how about opening the door so I can get out of here?"

"Certainly." Day watched Jing bend to his workstation and waited for the huge doors separating the base from the outside world to rumble open. "You're clear," the creature said presently. "May your voyage be profitable."

"Thanks. See you soon," Bonnie said. "Okay, computer. Take us into a standard parking orbit."

"Certainly, Bonnie. I'm designed to take you anywhere in known space. No knowledge of astrogation is necessary on your part. I have all co-ordinates in memory, along with the required navigational information including appropriate Jump points. Just tell me where, and I'll whisk you there!"

"You sound like a commercial."

"Sorry. I didn't mean to offend."

"You didn't. I was kidding."

"You have a sense of humor, then. I'll alter my programming accordingly. I'm used to the one called Auntie."

"You have my sympathy," Day said, dryly. "Give me the view forward, please."

The main screen changed to comply with Day's request. She watched as the Xannyk lifted from the hangar floor and glided gently through the opening and into a wide tunnel lit only by strips of blue guide lights. The ground sloped sharply upwards and as the Xannyk neared the far end another door slid out of the way and the ship popped out from the cool, underground gloom and into the blazing afternoon.

The sight of the desert reminded Day she must stink something awful and that a good bath was undoubtedly in order. In a minute... "Gimme a rear view, please." The screen's image dissolved to one of the tunnel door closing behind the departing yacht. Day noted without surprise that it was well camouflaged, looking for all intents and purposes like part of the rock outcropping surrounding it, designed to confound all but the most thorough snoops.

Traffic was heavy heading spaceward and Day watched with satisfaction as the Xannyk brazenly bullied its way between a commercial ship and a smaller yacht, flicking itself into position with an élan many living pilots wouldn't have touched. "Nice maneuver," she commented.

Was that a condescending sniff that Day heard? "Of course, Bonnie," the computer said matter of factly. "I'm a Xannyk." Then, as if to maintain a computer's normal tone of servitude, "Of course I've never seen you fly, so you could very well be a better pilot than I."

"Could be," Day replied, "But I wouldn't want to bet on it. Tell you what. Forget about that parking orbit. Can you take me straight to where the QUEEN VICTORIA is?"

There was the briefest of pauses as the computer electronically mulled over the question. "I match its last known position in your personal file Daylight One. I can estimate where it is now, assuming it hasn't changed course."

"Thank you. Please take me there."

"Consider it done. We will arrive at where the QUEEN VICTORIA should be in approximately 45 hours."

"Good. Keep me informed. I'm going to have a bath." Day got up and headed for the head.

The Xannyk was designed to "cradle two-to-four people in the lap of luxury," according to the brochures, and was fully equipped for long voyages. Aft of the bridge, and connected to it by both an archway and a pass-through, was the galley, the microscopic size of which belied its capabilities. Farther back were the twin cabins, each with its own bed, dresser/mirror and storage area. Between them, and accessible from both bedrooms and the short corridor to them, was the head, a state-of-the-art refreshing center that had been called "positively decadent" by some technophobe group when the original version had debuted on the big Xannyk Saloon a few years back. The comment had since appeared in the company's advertising, accenting the word "positively" in a way that made it seem like a compliment. Day whistled appreciatively when she saw what was in store for her and began wriggling out of her filthy clothes.

An hour later she was feeling human again and ready to tackle the assignment. She dressed in a loose robe and went back to the bridge, plopping onto the overstuffed couch. She asked for a status report.

"We are on course for the QUEEN VICTORIA," the computer said. "Our first Jump will be in ten hours."

"Good. Load file Daylight One, please."

"Password, please."

"Heebie Jeebies." The monitor screen came to life with the Club logo, which faded away to black after a few seconds. Day told the computer to bring her up to date with what was known about the QUEEN VICTORIA incident, and lines of text began scrolling up the screen, following her eye movement to keep it timed with her reading speed.

There was little in the file to help her. Communication with the liner had been cut off abruptly and never reestablished. What confirmed foul play, as opposed to random chance, was a ransom demand that had arrived on both Ramallah and Bolingnar within seconds of each other, delivered mere hours after contact was broken with the liner. Day wondered what had happened to the time honored kidnapping tradition of making the victims and their people sweat for a while, to soften them up, make them listen to reason? Did no one have patience any more?

Her eyes widened when she read the ransom demand: whoever

had done the deed wanted twenty per cent of the net planetary product, for each planet, for the past standard year. As the itemized account provided showed, it was a very tidy sum. "Money?" Day asked no one in particular. "Who just asks for money?" Traditionally, in acts of terrorism like that, the perpetrators always wanted something political, like the freeing of prisoners or the exchange of hostages, the end of peace talks, whatever. "Computer, how did the ransom demands get to the two planets?"

"Drone pods, Bonnie. Nothing unusual about them."

"Were they analyzed?"

"The races in question went over them with what you'd call a fine tooth comb and found nothing to hint of where they came from. Of course, their methods of detection aren't as good as those available in other places."

"So I suspected. What do you think? Would it be worthwhile for us to have them examined?"

"Possibly, though from the data in the file it doesn't look like there'd be much to find anyway. If I might make a suggestion...."

"Suggest away."

"If you do want an analysis performed, it would probably be more efficient to order it through the Club. I feel it would be a waste of time going to either planet, at least with the information we currently have."

"You think we should keep heading for the ship?"

"Definitely. That is where the crime was perpetrated and that is where any clues should be."

"I agree." To hell with the drones. Whoever had pulled off this stunt was obviously well prepared and Day doubted there'd be anything to find on the pods. If worse came to worst, she'd tell Auntie to have them looked at, like the computer suggested.

"Is there any information to link the disappearances of the other Supra agents with the QUEEN VICTORIA incident?"

"No, other than the fact that Supra 4 was on board the QUEEN VICTORIA."

"Let me see the file anyway." The new information appeared on the screen, and Day scanned it quickly. No help there. The other agents' disappearances couldn't be tied to the QUEEN VICTORIA, though Day felt Auntie was right to smell a rat. The timing was just too convenient.

Day found it hard to believe there was no political motivation behind the attack. It just didn't make sense otherwise. She called up a review of the area's recent politics. The peace negotiations, what with the well-known attitudes and behavior of the races involved, had been shaky from the start. The protagonist planets, which lay third and fourth from their primary sun, had been at odds since being introduced to each other via old fashioned radio in the days before they had attained spaceflight. Later, after having rained warheads on each other for a century or so, neither side was in a particularly forgiving or co-operative mood.

If it hadn't been for contact from the Co-operative, Day thought, and the advantages federation with such a far reaching body promised, the Ramallans and Bolingnaria would probably never have begun talking at all. As it had worked out, the peace emissaries had been sent on a "working vacation" cruise of the sector, in what was to have been their first, exploratory bargaining session. Day wondered how the talks had been going.

But there was nothing to indicate any factions angry at the way events were unfolding had been upset enough, or smart enough, to pull off the kidnapping. Let alone the decimation of the Club. Day finished the file and closed it. The monitor went blank.

"Looks like I'm on my own," she said. "Figures." That meant there was nothing to do except review what she knew and hope she'd think of something new, until they reached the QUEEN VICTORIA. "Do you play chess?" she asked.

"Of course. Do you want to be red or white?"

"Red. How's your music library?"

"I'm a Xannyk."

"Good. Let's have Townshend's first opera." She settled back onto the couch as the chessboard appeared on the monitor and the first chords began playing from hidden speakers. The computer made its first move. "Queen's knight to Queen Bishop Three." Her piece strode around the neighboring pieces and took up its new position.

# DERELICT DUTY -- Chapter 5

"I must say, she certainly doesn't look like she's in very good shape, does she?" asked the computer, rather rhetorically, as it displayed the QUEEN VICTORIA on its monitor. The big liner was about five hundred kilometers ahead of the Xannyk. She was obviously a derelict: her airlocks gaped and, from the angle at which Day was approaching, the hole torn in the hull was a vicious clue as to what had happened. That, coupled with a lack of the normal interior illumination that was usually visible through the ports, sent an ominous message.

It had been an uneventful trip from Gault. The only remarkable thing had been Day's pleasure at how the new Xannyk minimized the gut wrenching feeling that accompanied a hyperspace Jump. Instead of her organs feeling as if they were boiling dry from the inside, she had experienced only a slight flip-flop in her stomach before the new sky replaced the old one on the viewscreen. It was hardly more than the sensation one got from a stall in a winged atmospheric flyer. "Nice jump," she'd commented, to which the computer replied with some recorded sales pitch on how that type of yacht "reduced Jump Impact Trauma to virtual nonexistence." Day ordered the spiel shut off before it made her vomit.

"You can say that again," Day breathed as she leaned forward in her chair peering at the image of the liner. "What do you make of it?"

"H.V QUEEN VICTORIA, no possibility of doubt," said the computer. "It matches the records, except for the damage of course, and it is exactly where it should be."

"That's it?"

"Well, it has obviously been depressurized from the main lock to the bridge, at least as far back as the first sets of airtight doors. A large area of the ship may still be intact, since there appears to be little other damage to the hull itself."

"Hmm. Any chance of survivors?" It would save her a lot of legwork if she could get some decent information right from the horse's mouth, so to speak. But from the look of things, someone had shut down the ship's main power supply, throwing Life Support onto emergency batteries. They would have worn out long ago.

The computer echoed her pessimism. "I doubt it. While there's an excellent chance someone may have survived the initial attack, I calculate a less than one per cent chance of finding even a single survivor now."

"That's what I figured." Well, you couldn't have everything. Day resigned herself to a long and unpleasant reconnaissance of the liner starting with the bridge, from where she could access to the main computer.

"Computer, analyze that hole on the bridge and see if it's big enough for me to get through."

"Three meters in diameter, Bonnie, almost exactly. Plenty of room for you and your suit."

"Good. Prepare my suit, please."

"Okay. I doubt you'll find anyone on the bridge, though, Bonnie. Explosive decompression would have sent any personnel into space."

"I know, but if someone from outside hit the ship, which the hole in the hull would suggest to me, the bridge would be the ideal place to strike first. You've got control over almost everything." Day felt sure that was how it had happened. There could also have been help from stooges inside the QUEEN VICTORIA but, either way, a quick, decisive blow aimed at the bridge would be the most efficient way to attack.

"An interesting theory," said the computer, "And I must admit it fits the few facts we have at hand."

"How long before we're alongside?"

"Approaching now. I assume you want to match orbits?"

"Of course. We'll be here for a few hours at least. Pull alongside, about fifty meters off, and face the airlock toward the QUEEN VICTORIA."

"The course has been computed. The power up sequence in your spacesuit is now complete and everything checks out, so you can exit whenever you wish."

"Good. Thanks."

"I don't know if the suit radio will carry from inside the ship," Day said as she slid the space helmet over her head. "It should be okay from the bridge, but once I get deep into passenger country I can't guarantee you'll be able to pick me up." She fastened the helmet with its characteristic twist and click motion and heard the soft hiss as the air supply turned on automatically. A cool breeze began wafting against her cheek. It was a touch too cool for her liking, and she twisted her head and wiggled her chin onto the thermostat control, adjusting it to her preferred temperature.

"I'll keep monitoring anyway. I don't feel right being out of contact."

"You and me both! I don't expect to run into anything but ghosts aboard this ship, though, so I wouldn't worry too much about it." Day finished with the suit, ran through the checks. Satisfied, she plugged the wristcom into the connection on her waist. "Okay, let's get the show on the road. Open the inner door, please."

The Xannyk complied and Day entered the airlock. The door shut behind her. She felt the space suit stiffen slightly as the atmosphere drained from the little room. The outer door slid open silently and Day stepped into the void, facing the huge bulk of the QUEEN VICTORIA a short distance away from her. She floated in a rather aimless manner as her minimal inertia propelled her into the open space between the ships. She began a slow rotating motion, but quickly arrested it with her suit thrusters. She wriggled around until she pointed toward the liner's shattered bridge, then shot a quick blast from her thrusters and propelled herself toward it.

As she neared, she noticed that the hole in the hull was a nice, clean rupture. Day knew of dozens of weapons and tools capable of such precise destruction. Day reversed her direction of thrust and came to rest at the hole. As she poked her helmeted head through it she noticed only minimal damage to the bridge. A competent job.

"At least the fail-safes worked properly," Day mumbled after squeezing through the hole, noticing that the airtight bulkhead had operated as designed.

"It doesn't seem to have helped," remarked the Xannyk's computer from the speaker near Day's left ear. "By the way, as you can undoubtedly tell, I can still read you."

"Good. Are you getting visual, too?" She moved her head around so the video pickup on the forehead of her helmet would get a clear view to send back to the yacht.

"Good resolution and color."

"Excellent. I see Jing's improved on his earlier version." She continued panning around the bridge. "It's not hard to figure out what happened here, is it?"

A chill went up and down Day's spine. She'd seen death enough not to be queasy about it. But that didn't make the thought of being blown out into space helpless any more pleasant, especially knowing full well that the first breath your body would force you to take before your screaming lungs burst would be the last thing you ever did. The concept of drowning in anything, be it vacuum, water, whatever, had never appealed to her. It stemmed from a childhood incident she'd all but forgotten, except in her nightmares. She shuddered and put the thought away. "Let's get to work."

The QUEEN VICTORIA's computer I/O port was on the left side of the console. Day went over to it and patched in her own computer. She booted the system. The little screen on the inner surface of her helmet sparkled to life above her head and a menu appeared. A sweet contralto voice sang into Day's ear "Hello. How can I serve you?"

"I want you to download all the log files from the remote computer," Day said.

"All the files? That will take a lot of storage."

"Don't you have enough memory?"

"Of course I do. I was just informing you of the size of the task."

"Then do it." She unsnapped the computer and clipped it onto the bridge console and went over to the bank of gauges on the opposite side of the control panel. "How long will it take?"

"Eight minutes, seventeen seconds." Time to look around, not that there was much to see. She spent a few minutes on the gauges, making sure good video of them was getting back to the Xannyk.

"Make anything out of these?" Day asked. She couldn't, but she wasn't a spaceship expert. The Xannyk, on the other hand, had in its memory the operations of every standard model of ship in the Cooperative.

"There's nothing remarkable," replied the yacht. "The controls are as you'd expect to find."

"Which is?"

"Batteries are down, main drive off, life support inoperative. Shall I continue?"

"No." She was a powered-down derelict, though she could undoubtedly be reactivated by jump-starting the drive, a pointless undertaking at this point in time. It would take hours before the fuel mix would be rich enough to even power up the lights now that the batteries were dead, dead, dead. Day wanted to be long gone by then.

But it meant slogging through the dark in a spacesuit. That wouldn't make the trip particularly pleasant, but it beat sticking around the ship of death. If there were any gems of information to be discovered aboard the QUEEN VICTORIA, they would probably come from the data she was downloading.

After a few more minutes, the wristcom meekly called for her attention.

"Finished?"

"Yes. I've downloaded six point one three four seven Googolbytes."

"Good. Have you got enough room to make a backup?"

"No. May I suggest you upload the data into another computer?"

"I'll do just that. Save everything and park."

Time to get the rest of the lonely deathwatch over with. She disconnected the little computer and re-stowed it. "I'm coming out now." She took a last look around, then moved back to the hole that led outside. She went back into open space, making her way to the still gaping emergency airlock. She went inside.

As she'd expected, the trip through the QUEEN VICTORIA wasn't pleasant. At least the liner hadn't gone down without a fight. Day thought the crew had done a pretty good job of defending her considering she was a commercial ship not really equipped for battle despite whatever precautions may have been taken to protect the dubiously valuable cargo.

"It doesn't look like anyone survived," she said. It was pitch dark inside the liner, with not even emergency lighting active. Cold too, judging by the frost. The spotlight on her helmet sliced through the black-death, bringing into horrifically blazing view the bodies scattered throughout the interior, floating bizarrely in the zero gravity environment. Many of the bodies, especially the ones she came across closest to the airlock, had been shot. Others had obviously died later. The sights made Day progressively more depressed the deeper she ventured through the QUEEN VICTORIA's labyrinth of corridors and companionways.

"Computer? Are you still getting this?" She guessed not, since there was no reply. So all the data she was collecting automatically through the suit/sensor/Xannyk link was uselessly spewing into the vacuum. Oh, well, at least it was being saved in her onboard computer. Besides, there hadn't been anything to see. Whoever had knocked over the ship had been thorough and professional. Mercenaries?

Or pirates? Piracy was common enough in some of the rougher sectors, but pirates were normally after some immediate award, something tangible and liquid they could haul away with them and spend or sell. They tended to hit freighters or the occasional colony, not mess with a passenger ship and waste time keeping hostages alive until they could be bailed out. Terrorists, then? Some fanatics devoted to an idiotic cause who wanted to show the galaxy that they had a divine vision of how things should be run? She wouldn't rule out some group. Excessive zeal for a particular principle had a habit throughout history of causing incidents like the one she was investigating.

Still, it didn't seem right. The hostage takers wanted money, not political favors.

That still made mercenaries the most logical choice. Day could only hope that logic, however twisted, would have some bearing on the actions of the perpetrators.

The beam from her spotlight picked up a widening of the corridor and the extra open space, where the walls were far enough away to keep them hidden from her light, made her feel even more closed in. There was a wide opening just ahead, and from what Day could see it looked like a dining room, a bar, or some place like that. Day went in, adjusting her light so it would illuminate as much of the room as possible.

It was a passenger lounge, littered with tables and chairs floating crazily in the space, scorched by weapon bursts from the battle that had obviously happened there. Day smiled grimly, in spite of herself. Now she had a good idea of where the last stand had been made, and how it had gone, though what good the knowledge would do her was doubtful.

Day noticed the mess in the lounge hadn't been caused only by the fighting. Some survivors of the attack had chosen to spend their last few hours in a fog of zero gee intoxication. There was vomit and blood from several different, and generally mutually incompatible, species all over the place, big disgusting globules floating here and there. Broken bottles and glasses would have made moving about quite dangerous if Day hadn't been protected by her spacesuit. Her stomach was in danger of turning at the sight; she had a strong urge to leave, to rocket screaming through the passageways, up the decks and out the airlock to the warm comfort of the Xannyk.

Ashamed at her weakness, Day tried to stifle the feeling, to bury it deep inside her again, but the oppressive darkness and oppressing sense of death made it difficult. She hovered at one end of the room for a moment, taking deep breaths and slowing her heart, calling on her experience to give her control again.

She shuddered, and the motion moved her sideways as a blaster beam cut through the darkness where she'd been a half second earlier. She whirled around, cutting in her thrusters as she reached for the blaster at her side. She panned her helmet around, and the spotlight picked up a shadowy figure just inside the lounge's entrance arch. It was tracking her with its own blaster.

Day maneuvered to the opposite side as the gun went off and again the beam just missed. She returned fire, but the figure slipped from her light and was lost in the blackness. Frantically, she swung her head from side to side. Nothing. She doused the light.

"Where the hell did this guy come from?" she muttered under her breath.

"You were lucky getting away from us the first time, Day" a male voice said. "You won't be so lucky again." His suit's spotlight came on and swept the room. Day hid behind one of the larger tables that floated near one bulkhead. The beam passed by her. "Look, I got lots of air, so I can wait as long as you can," the other person said. "So why don't you come out now and save us both a lot of trouble?"

Day ignored the suggestion and, after another sweep of the room, the man shut off the light. Dammit, Day thought. As long as he'd kept his light on, she'd had the advantage and could have picked him off easily, given the chance to squeeze off a shot. Now that the darkness was back, they were on an even playing field.

Time to do something. Day turned her head to the left and wiggled her nose against a switch on the helmet's interior. A pair of snoopers snapped down inside the faceplate. She pressed her face into them, moving her head slightly to make the eyepieces fit properly. She peeked over the table and scanned the lounge, looking for the energy signature from her enemy's suit thrusters.

There it was! A faint constellation of smudgy glows on the other side of the room twinkled as their owner moved around. From the way they were moving, it looked as if the guy was effectively blind, and he wasn't much of a searcher, either. At least he'd figured out that he should keep quiet to prevent her from homing in on his radio signal.

Day raised her blaster, her body tensing, her breathing rate increasing slightly. She took aim and turned on her spotlight. Her opponent was facing away from her just then, but with the appearance of the light, spun toward her. Day let go a maximum blast. In the circle of illumination, Day could see an amazed look on the man's face as his helmet ruptured and half his head was blasted away. He released his gun from his grip and began floating away as he grew still except for a sickening twitching of his limbs. After a few seconds even that stopped and he merely floated, revolving and oozing slowly and sickeningly.

Day went to the body and examined it. She couldn't tell much about the man because what was exposed through the space suit was a semi-spherical bloody mass of half blasted head. She turned her attention to the spacesuit. It was a standard model, but finished in a deep, glossy black instead of the usual bright, easy-to-see-in-space colors. It was unusual, but wouldn't teach her anything about the man or his organization, just that they liked camouflage. She pushed the disrupted body away from her.

There was nothing to learn inside the QUEEN VICTORIA; it was just a dead hulk, some corporate insurance claim. It was time to leave.

After what seemed like a year, she recognized the passageway that led to the emergency airlock, and a few seconds later was in open space. She turned toward the Xannyk, then stopped, a shocked look on her face as she viewed the yacht.

It looked like a miniature version of the QUEEN VICTORIA, floating dead in space, a substantial hole torn in the airlock.

# XANNYK PANIC -- Chapter 6

"Great," Day muttered. "Just great. So much for my ride." She moved across the space between the ships, and took a good look at the yacht.

Fortunately, the damage wasn't as severe as it looked, but it was enough to throw a monkey wrench into things. A good portion of the outer airlock door had been blasted away, which meant she'd have to bleed the whole ship of its atmosphere if she expected to get back in. Not a fatal problem, but a royal pain nonetheless. She wondered why the damage had been so limited. Perhaps her attacker had had eyes on the yacht for himself, or maybe he wasn't nearly as thorough as he thought. Whatever. She filed it away for later consideration.

"Computer?"

"Bonnie!" the computer positively shouted from Day's speaker. "I'm extremely pleased to hear that you're alive!"

"That makes two of us, friend," Day replied dryly. "What happened?"

"Well, I was reviewing all the data you'd sent back from the QUEEN VICTORIA before I lost your signal, then that other ship arrived. I tried to warn you, but of course you were too far inside." Day swiveled about to look for the other ship; it was hanging a few hundred meters above the QUEEN VICTORIA out of sight of the airlock through which she'd entered the liner. It was a two person deep space shuttle, black-painted like her attacker's space suit had been; a comfortable enough vessel for hopping around space, but hardly any competition for the Xannyk when it came to creature comforts and performance. She hoped it was empty.

"Computer, have you scanned that ship?"

"Of course."

"Did it come with two passengers or one?"

"Only one person left it and my scanners haven't picked up any signs of life since. I'm sorry," Day pictured an electronic shrugging of shoulders, "but that doesn't prove anything."

"That figures." Day pulled her weapon out of its stowage pocket and headed for the little ship. "What's your status" she said to the Xannyk. "How badly damaged are you?"

"Superficially, Bonnie. Just a rupture in the outer airlock door. The person was obviously in a hurry and must have just wanted to keep you from getting back in."

"Can it be fixed here? Or do we need to ground somewhere?"

"Temporary repairs won't present any problems, Bonnie. I have all the tools necessary. If I might suggest, use one of the airtight doors from the interior. The one from the spare bedroom will suffice more than adequately."

"Good."

"Of course that will make the room unsafe in case of decompression."

"That's okay. I'm only using one bedroom anyway." Day reached the sleek, needle-nosed, black shuttle, its outer door still open to the void. Day took that to be a good sign that there was probably no one else inside. Just in case, she raised her blaster before going into the airlock and aimed it at the inner door. She started the lock cycling and could feel the increasing resistance against her suit as air flooded into the tiny compartment. When the green light went on over the inner door, it slid open, whether automatically or at the urging of someone inside she couldn't tell.

Blaster ready, Day peeked into the cramped interior of the little craft. Even from inside the lock she could tell the ship was empty. The bridge also functioned as sleeping quarters and galley and, besides the head, represented all there was to see inside. Unless someone was using the facilities, the shuttle was abandoned.

Day relaxed and re-slung the gun. She went inside and checked the head. It was empty. She spent a few minutes looking over the belongings of the man she'd killed inside the QUEEN VICTORIA. He definitely wasn't a good housekeeper, judging from the clothes lying around the place. It reminded her of her younger brother's bedroom back when they'd lived together. There was a fully stocked weapons cabinet in its usual location on the rear bulkhead, full of typical ordnance.

Day finished her inspection and went back outside. She found nothing to indicate who the man was or, more importantly, where he was from and who had sent him.

"Are your tanks large enough to hold your air supply?" she asked when she was once again outside the Xannyk. She'd have to either store the atmosphere inside while the inner door was opened or dump it all into space. She preferred the former; breathing vacuum wasn't her idea of a fun way to spend an afternoon. She'd seen enough examples of it aboard the QUEEN VICTORIA to reinforce that opinion. She considered, for about a second, abandoning the Xannyk and riding in the little shuttle, but preferred the surroundings of the Xannyk for obvious reasons.

"No, Bonnie."

"Can you override the airtight doors?"

"Yes, if you order me to. Why?"

Day looked at the oxygen level indicator on the left forearm of her suit. She'd better get a move on or she'd be breathing vacuum right there. "Because I want you to put it in place right now. Then I want you to bleed as much air as possible from the bridge and pump it into the aft compartment on the other side of the door. Understand?"

"Of course! Increase the amount of air aft and decrease it in the bridge so you don't lose as much. That's pretty smart, Bonnie!"

"That's why they pay me the big bucks. Can you do all that?"

"Definitely. Are you ordering me to?"

"No, I'm just planning your next redesign. Of course I'm ordering you to! Start now. I'm getting low on pressure myself out here."

"Beginning." Day had to take the computer's word that it was performing the operation as ordered, since from outside nothing could be seen. While she waited she noticed with dismay that, besides her dwindling air supply, she'd developed one of those itches that always come at the worst possible times and places. This one was in the small of her back, deep inside the space suit. Getting out of the rig couldn't come soon enough for her.

Presently she heard "Airtight door deployed." Shortly after that came "Bridge oxygen pressure at one per cent. Aft pressure off the scale. I'd say we're ready."

"Good."

What was left of the outer door rolled open silently, and Day could see into the bridge. She scrambled inside and punched the button that would reseat the inner door. It closed.

"Okay, pressurize," she said, "And fast!"

Air rushed back onto the bridge. After a while the airtight door opened and Day knew it was safe. Her gloved fingers tore at the seals of her helmet and, removing it, she drank in the atmosphere and reveled in the open space of the bridge, pleased to be free of the "fishbowl hat."

"Thanks," she said after taking several deep breaths. "That worked well."

"Yes. It was a good plan. We can do it again when you patch the airlock."

"Which I'd better get doing."

"There's no rush, Bonnie," the computer pointed out. "You can take care of it any time before our next jump." That was true, Day admitted, and there were equally important things to get done, like uploading her portable computer into the yacht. Having only one functioning airlock door was strictly against spacecraft regulations, and could be darn dangerous to boot, but she had confidence in the Xannyk and if it was confident she'd take the risk.

"Now *you've* had a good idea," Day said, shrugging herself out of the spacesuit. When she was free of it, she picked it up, smoothed it, and hung it in its closet near the airlock, plugging it into the charger. A green light came on; the suit would be replenished while it was in storage. Day pried the little computer from its mount on the suit and shut the closet. She took it to the Xannyk's main console, plugged it in, and booted it. "Here you go," she said. "Download to your heart's content."

"Consider it done, Bonnie," said the Xannyk. "I'll analyze the data as it transfers."

Day realized she was terribly hungry and headed for the galley. "Good. How 'bout rustling me up a nice omelet, too? Say, three eggs, ham, cheese, 'shrooms? And lots of garlic?"

"Certainly. Coming right up."

In the galley, Day inserted a plate into the cook'n'munch, then set a fork onto the tabletop. She got a glass of cold water and leaned against the counter. A minute later, the steaming meal slid out of the cook'n'munch. In typically thoughtful Xannyk fashion, the omelet was accompanied by two thick, well-buttered slices of dark toast. Day grabbed a pair of hot handlers, picked up the plate, and set it on the table.

She'd just dug in when the Xannyk announced it had finished downloading. A little later, she mopped up the last bits of omelet with the final crumbs of toast and washed them down with water. She got up and put the dishes in the cleaner, then went back onto the bridge and fell roughly onto the couch.

"So what have you got for me?" she asked, flicking the button on the coffee table to zoom the monitor's magnification setting.

"I haven't had time to correlate everything," the computer replied. "After all, there are weeks of records there. However," the screen dissolved to a view of space, "I started my analysis by going backwards from the point at which the recording cuts off. The last few moments of the visual navigation log are quite interesting."

"Let's see 'em." The computer ran the video clip made by the QUEEN VICTORIA'S automatic recorders. The first few moments, shot from the upper hull array, simply showed the body of the ship as it stretched aft from the recorder's vantage point, backed by the stars; Day found herself leaning forward to get a better view of the screen as the liner was joined by another ship. The video quality was excellent, and Day watched in horrified fascination as the new ship sparkled out of hyperspace far closer to the liner than she'd have expected from her experience, approached the liner, opened, and sent a blast to a point forward of the recorder, out of view. It must have made the hole she had entered the bridge through.

She gasped in spite of herself as she witnessed the next stage of the attack, carried out soundlessly before her as the black ship blasted the main airlock. The army of black suited figures deployed around the liner and the tube started to extend between the ships. Then, suddenly, the recording ended. Day let out a whistle.

"I'm sorry, Bonnie, that's when the automatic recording stopped. It looks interesting, though, doesn't it?"

Day sat quietly for a moment, thinking about what she'd just witnessed. She nodded. "Possibly. Can you identify that ship?"

"Surely. Just a moment." Day drummed her fingers impatiently on the arm of the sofa. "Well, it matches my records of a Class IV freighter, but that doesn't make sense."

"Why?"

The computer told her about that type of freighter's normal inability to use hyperspace, ending the short lecture by saying "And according to the log you just saw, that ship arrived out of hyperspace. That's the only way it could appear like that, as if out of nothing. Otherwise it would have been visible as a point of light in the distance until it got close enough to make out. I'm confused."

"Why couldn't that freighter have been retrofitted with a hyperdrive? Or some kind of invisibility screen?"

"No reason, I guess. The first is an impractical conversion, though, when there are already so many types of vessels already capable of hyperspace. The second is beyond my technological knowledge."

"Could whoever did this have needed this type of ship specifically, or just wanted this type because it suited their purposes. Maybe they just wanted to throw people off track. Who knows?" She reached her hands up to the top of her head and rubbed them through her mane.

"Certainly not I, Bonnie," said the computer. "I'm the best ship's computer private money can buy, but my reasoning powers still fall short of a human's."

"I've known a few humans you'd probably beat. Don't worry about it. Maybe they'll upgrade you in the next model." Day put her hands behind her head and knitted her fingers together. She leaned back on the couch and stared at the ceiling. After a minute or two she ordered the computer to display the technical drawings of a Class IV freighter and the computer obediently put them on the big screen. Day studied them intently.

"Makes sense to me," she said at last. A Class IV freighter was big enough to serve many purposes, yet small and common enough to avoid notice if it didn't flaunt its extraordinary capabilities. It would make an ideal Trojan horse type of battleship, once it gained the range and striking advantages of hyperdrive and if some of the cargo holds were converted to living space. She marveled at the ingenuity of it all. Whoever was behind this was good.

By allowing the QUEEN VICTORIA's log to remain, however, Day's quarry had left a trail that, with luck, she could follow. She ordered the schematics off the screen and turned her gaze back to the ceiling. "Computer, how are those freighters sold?"

"I don't understand, Bonnie."

Day frowned. "I mean how do people, or companies, buy them? Do they deal directly with the manufacturer? Do they go through dealerships or agents? How would whoever knocked over the QUEEN VICTORIA have gotten a hold of that freighter?"

"Just a minute," the Xannyk replied. "Class IV freighters are very common for intra-system shipping throughout the Co-operative and the one in question could have been bought and sold on the used market. We may never trace it."

"Garbage. Anything can be traced if you try hard enough and if you look in the right places, or grease the right palms." She thought for a moment. "Where are the ships made?"

"Scree DiPont. A company called Stornoway Enterprises. Its manufacturing facilities for space vehicles are there."

"Then that's where we have to go. Somewhere they'll have a

record of that ship."

"Are you sure? The freighter could be very old."

"Hopefully it won't matter. There's an old law dating back from when governments downsized their bureaucracies. Back before they built newer and more bloated ones. Instead of having a Department of Space Vehicles or something like that, individual manufacturers were required to keep records for Government inspection, outlining the history of their products. Subsequent sales were listed in the records, too. So far as I know that law has never been repealed." She realized the ship could have been bought on the black market, too, but there was no point in crossing that bridge until she had to.

"Then shall I set course for Scree DiPont?"

"You can calculate the course and get ready, but we should repair that door. Tell you what. Compose a report telling Auntie what we've found so far, then squirt it off to headquarters." Day grabbed her blaster and started aft. "I'll cut off a piece of door to patch with."

The repair was accomplished without mishap, though Day had to re-meld the patch to the door at some places because the molecules hadn't set properly the first time. Once the menial task was finished, she had the ship open and close the door several times before she came back in, to ensure the patch wouldn't cause friction by rubbing against the ship.

"Judging from the specifications of a repair like that, assuming you did it correctly," the Xannyk commented, "There should be no problem with the airlock holding pressure."

"Don't worry your pretty little processors about the quality of my work," Day replied. She came back into the lock, began its cycle, and started removing her helmet as the air flooded back in; by the time the inner door slid open, she had the seals broken and was twisting the fishbowl hat from its mounting ring. She went inside and finished getting out of the spacesuit, then stowed it back in its cradle and plugged it in. "Now let's head for Scree DiPont. But first, grab onto that shuttle with a tow beam and bring it along." She didn't know how, but had a nagging feeling that the shuttle could come in handy later.

"Done. We're off," said the Xannyk. Day lay down on the couch, on her side, to watch the main screen. The display was of the view outside and, as the yacht began moving Day could see the QUEEN VICTORIA get nearer, then pass out of sight as the Xannyk went over it, turning in a three dimensional arc onto its projected course. The yacht came to within some fifty meters of the big liner, then it was gone as the Xannyk headed toward its first Jump.

"How long until we get to Scree DiPont?"

"We jump in one-point-five days. Downflight after that will be three days. For your information, we'll be coming into the system from outside the plane of the ecliptic."

"Good." Day yawned, got up, and headed aft. "I'm going to bed," she called out. "Keep processing those logs from the QUEEN and give me a progress report when I wake up."

"Would you like me to wake you at any particular time?"

"Not unless something happens you think I should know about. Okay?"

"Fine, Bonnie. Pleasant dreams."

"Thanks." She entered the sleeping quarters, stripped off her clothing, and dove for the covers. She was asleep almost before her eyes closed.

# RUMINATIONS AND CALCULATIONS -- Chapter 7

Bonnie Day slept a troubled sleep peppered with nightmares. A recurring theme was that she was floating weightlessly through an old-fashioned churchyard cemetery, while rotting corpses reached out of the ground to grab at her legs and haul her down below the surface of the earth. Gasping desperately for breath, she struggled wildly in panic as the ghostly hands tugged and tore at her, while the loud, angry hissing of an oxygen leak assaulted her subconsciousness. Three times she awoke with a start, drenched in a cold sweat. Her body was tired to the very core, but her mind wouldn't rest.

"Excuse me, Bonnie," the computer said gently. Day stopped fidgeting and sat up, grateful for the interruption.

"What is it?"

"I'm sorry to be so inquisitive," the computer said, "But I can't help noticing you're having trouble getting to sleep. Is something bothering you?"

Day frowned. "Nothing you can do anything about, old friend. No offense."

"None taken. I can't be offended anyway. But maybe I can help. Would you like me to sing for you?"

Day smiled wryly. "You mean sing me a lullaby? That's cute."

"It could be a lullaby or a symphony; whatever you want. Naturally I can provide the sound of any combination of musical instruments you might want."

"Naturally. Sure, go ahead."

"Thank you. What would you like to hear?"

"I don't know." Day thought for a moment. "Something light and quiet, I guess." She got up, went to the head, and opened the first-aid cabinet. She took out a soporific tab and washed it down with some water, then returned to bed.

"How's this?" The room filled with soft, pastoral music that reminded Day of sunny afternoons on a warm planet, of lying on the grass imagining outrageous imaginary shapes in the clouds. It made her feel good.

"That's just fine. Thank you."

"My pleasure, Bonnie. I hope it works."

Day curled into fetal position and closed her eyes. "You and me both. 'Night."

"Pleasant dreams, Bonnie."

"No dreams, with any luck." The music, abetted by the drug, caressed and soothed her. Soon consciousness slipped away and she slept once more. This time the haunted dreams stayed away. When she finally awoke, she was surprised to find sixteen hours had passed. The music still played softly, a different selection than the one she remembered hearing before. She slipped from under the covers and stood up. The music stopped.

"Good morning, Bonnie," the Xannyk said. "I hope your sleep was pleasant."

"Very nice. Thanks for your help." Day yawned, bent down and touched her toes, then stretched up onto her tiptoes, repeating the exercise several times. "And please keep up the music, though I think something a little more lively would suit me better right now." She did a few jumping jacks, sit-ups, and a couple of isometric exercises against the bulkhead before hitting the shower. When she returned to the sleeping quarters she asked for a status report.

"I've finished analyzing the QUEEN VICTORIA's log files," the computer told her, "And unfortunately there's not really anything more to tell. Everything aboard the ship was perfectly normal until the freighter came out of hyperspace near it. You know what happened after that. I'm sorry, Bonnie."

"Don't be. I'm not really surprised, otherwise the VIC would have had time to send a distress call."

"What do we do now?"

"Carry on. We must be coming up to Jump pretty soon, aren't we?"

"Jump will occur in seventeen hours, five minutes, and four seconds."

"Any word from Club Headquarters?"

"Sorry."

Day dressed in a comfortable pair of shorts and a halter-top, then went forward to the bridge. "Turn on the screen, please. I'd like you to display all the information we have on the Stornoway company. Is there much?"

"Galactic almanac entries and assorted similar records. Company brochures of its products. Standard fare."

"Let me look at it anyway. Did you tell headquarters where we're going?" The computer replied in the affirmative. "Good. Now let's see what Stornoway is all about."

The computer was right; the information on the spaceship manufacturer was typical encyclopedia and advertising stuff. Stornoway was clean, a respected and successful corporation.

To the casual observer, their destination didn't appear to change visibly during the first hours after the hyperspace Jump. There was one glitch to the trip, however; the little shuttle had come loose from the tow beam when they popped back into normal space, and the Xannyk had to loop back and pick it up before resuming its original course. The extra maneuver was accomplished with little fuss, though it caused a delay and had the shuttle come loose at a different time it could have been lost. Day wondered if it was worth it dragging the thing along with them, but decided to continue for the present.

Eventually, Scree DiPont's star grew from being a mere pinpoint to a burning yellow glob, to a discernible and unwatchable disc. The Xannyk dropped toward her destination, the fourth planet out.

From what Day knew of Scree DiPont, she didn't expect a pleasant place to visit. Despite that, however, she looked forward to hitting groundside again, to breathing unbottled air and to walking more than a few meters at a time in any one direction. Besides, Scree DiPont would undoubtedly be a pleasant change from the bug-eyed, vomit covered, staring faces she'd found in the QUEEN VICTORIA, innocent victims of someone's mad plan. The thought of those helpless people made her angry, not only at the perpetrators, but at the line of work she'd reluctantly found herself involved in again. She longed to disappear into some quiet corner of the Co-operative. She'd had more than her fill of killing and of watching others die needlessly.

Damn that Auntie anyway! She had a lot of nerve hauling her back into the service. Sure, she could understand her dilemma, since there were no longer enough operatives around to do the job, but it was damn well time Auntie hired some more. It was all Auntie's fault for having recruited her in the first place. She'd sold her on the altruistic aspects of the job, the glory, the fast pace, the perks, and Day had been a kid looking for adventure. Auntie had somehow neglected to put things in their proper perspective, minimizing things like blood, terror, and deceit. The whole sales job had been a bill of goods and Day felt justified in wanting a refund.

So what if she'd have to look over her shoulder the rest of her life, watching for people with an axe to grind? She could handle that. She was smart, and with a new face and a new identity could start all over again, doing whatever she wanted. She'd just have to avoid places like Gault and stick to the boondocks, where she could disappear from sight. Like she should have this last time...

She growled unhappily and stood up. "Computer?"
"Yes, Bonnie?"
"Can you make scotch?"
"Yes, Bonnie."
"Good. Make me a double. Neat." She headed for the galley.

The mellowing effect of the liquor put Day into a better mood and, by the time they actually entered the Scree DiPont system, she was almost content with her lot in life. What the hell, she'd decided, this mission gave her the chance to pay back whoever'd killed all those people on the QUEEN VICTORIA, and all those other Supras, too. Then she'd tell Auntie she was through, again, and this time make it stick.

Her thoughts were interrupted by the Xannyk. "Approaching Scree DiPont's moon, Bonnie," it said. "I'm already in contact with planetary traffic control and am receiving landing instructions. Do you want to proceed?"

"Let's leave the shuttle in orbit around the moon," Day said, "Then we'll ground. These tired old feet are looking forward to being on dirt again. How far is the port from where Stornoway hangs out?"

The computer displayed a map. "The Stornoway complex is in Henning City, here..." A highlight appeared on the map, near its center. From there a line drew itself to a large circle several kilometers outside the city. "This is the nearest spaceport. It is not the main passenger traffic point of arrival and departure, but it is well used for commercial traffic. They may wonder why a Xannyk would be landing there," the computer pointed out.

"Why?" Day asked. "I'm just a socialite out to have repairs done on my ship. I may even want to buy a new one. I've got unlimited credit, you know, thanks to the Club, and I'm thinking about picking up a freighter 'cause I want something I can have made into a bigger yacht." She stood up and went aft to change into some 'street clothes.' "Go in for a standard approach and get a full service berth in the port." She thought of something. "Oh, and when you're talking to control tell them I want to hire a ground car. Something nice, like a landside version of you."

"Thanks for the compliment. I'll take care of everything. I assume you'd like a hotel?"

"Of course. Something big, expensive, and as decadent as possible."

The yacht grounded an hour later. It was late afternoon by the Scree DiPont clock, which ran on what they liked to call "digital time," consisting of ten hours broken down into a hundred minutes each. Through the monitor, Day could see the planet's star nearing the horizon, casting long shadows from the other grounded ships and the nearby buildings that made up the spaceport. An industrial haze hung over everything.

Day was dressed fashionably for Scree DiPont in a dark blue metacloth suit with thin, light blue stripes going down its length. It wasn't as comfortable as she liked, but this was the Scree DiPontians' home turf, and this attire would be noticed as fitting in with her rich playgirl cover. She looked at her watch ring, which she had adjusted for the local day. It was 6.5 hours.

"Did you get me a car?" she asked.

"A new Marshall Special awaits you outside the terminal," replied the computer. "By the way, you should try not to exert yourself too much for the first while."

"Thin atmosphere?"

"Thin and dirty, and higher gravity than that to which you've been accustomed while in me."

"Thanks. I'll be careful." She gave the Xannyk detailed instructions, including telling it to wait on standby, keeping a circuit peeled for her return, then made the ship repeat it all back to her. Satisfied that everything would be secure, she opened the airlock and went outside, onto the surface of Scree DiPont.

It stank. Day couldn't put her finger on what exactly the smell was, but it reminded her of dirty oil, used soiled underwear, and rotten eggs, all rolled into one. The air assaulted her nose and hurt her eyes and she began to wish she'd brought along her space suit. The sky of the heavily industrialized plant was already losing whatever luster it normally had. She could see clouds of chemical smoke rising from the not-too-distant Henning City, further choking things.

"So much for a walk in the sunshine," she said as she started toward the terminal a hundred meters or so in front of her. Once off the landing pad she stepped onto the slidewalk and was whisked toward the main building.

Compared with the last spaceport in which she'd been, Henning's was a dump. Where the New Las Vegas port had been ornate and gaudy to the extreme, this one was dull and grey and purely functional. Day thought it was going to be a strange sight to see a gleaming Marshall. It had better be gleaming, parked among what she imagined would be mostly grimy taxis, utility vehicles, and heavy haulers.

She was right. After having her identification stamped at Arrivals, she went immediately to Vehicle Pickup, identified herself and had her thumbprint fed into the reader. Then she went outside to the waiting transports and had no trouble finding her rented Marshall. It was parked by itself at the end of a long line of grey ground cabs; one space over from it began a line of dingy, battered buses.

She touched her thumb to the lock and the door opened upward with a gentle hissing. She threw her bag onto the passenger seat and slid behind the controls, noticing with satisfaction that it was a deluxe model. Good! Operating it would be as easy as talking, as long as she left it on auto drive.

The car didn't wait for her to speak, though. "Good afternoon, Miss," it said in a rather exotic-sounding male voice. "Would you care to go now?"

Day smiled at her reflection in the window. This, at least, was going to be pleasant.

"Yes. I'm registered at the Skypark Lodge."

"Thank you. It will take us forty five minutes to reach it."

"Isn't that a long time?"

"It's rush hour."

"That figures."

Despite being a slow, royal pain, the trip into Henning City was uneventful. The Marshall parked outside the hotel and Day went inside, leaving instructions with the robo-valet to park the car and have her luggage taken to her room.

She took a good, long look at the front of the hotel and wasn't thrilled with what she saw. While the Skypark Lodge may have been a five star hotel compared with what else was available on Scree DiPont, it would have only rated about two and a half in the Bonnie Day Guide to Galactic Hostelry. It was a dull, stone fronted building that rose some forty storeys above her, dirty windows holding the promise that whatever view there might be would almost certainly be worthless because of the filth that had built up on the outside.

Day was surprised to find a pleasant suite reserved for her, though it was smaller than she liked. It would suffice, especially since it was probably the best she'd find. Next order of business would be to find a place to eat, and she didn't feel like trying the so-called restaurant she'd passed in the lobby. She phoned the desk and was given directions to a quiet, local ethnic food restaurant the clerk said would probably suit her. She put on a light windbreaker and went downstairs to find the place.

She had only walked a few paces when she felt a firm tap on her shoulder. She turned and there in front of her stood a tall, four-armed creature whose origin escaped her. It was looking inquisitively at Day, two arms crossed in front of it and the other pair behind its back. "Excuse me, but are you Bonnie Day?" it asked in a wheezy, reedy voice.

"That depends," she said, wondering who could be looking for her already.

"Good," said the creature, ignoring the flip reply. "I thought it was you. Welcome to Henning City." Before Day had could react, the creature brought its second pair of arms from behind its back and Day got a quick glimpse of a stunner in its hand. She leapt backward, spun around, and started to roll sideways to the ground when she felt a numbing pain in her back. It spread through her body, bringing blackness.

She collapsed into a heap and lay still. The creature came closer and stood over her, laughing softly to itself.

# A FRIEND INDEED -- Chapter 8

When Bonnie Day awoke, her head pounded and throbbed with the pain that always accompanied a stunner attack. She was on some sort of bed, or a very comfortable floor. She opened her eyes and waited impatiently for things to come slowly into focus. In the back of her mind she was somewhat grateful for the pain; it meant she'd only been stunned, and not something far more permanent. She struggled onto one elbow and looked around at what she assumed was her prison.

It didn't look much like a prison. It was more like a hotel room. A video monitor took up most of the wall opposite her, and there was the usual complement of beds, chairs, and dressers. A door to Day's left led, presumably, into a bathroom.

There was a couch a meter or so from the bed on which she lay. The male human on it twisted around to stare back at her from his seat. He was blonde, with a light complexion, and Day immediately recognized the crooked smile. She groaned, shook her head, and sat up.

"What are you doing here, Mac?" His smile grew broader and he got up and came over to the bed. He reached out, took Day's hand, and shook it roughly. "Well, well, Bonnie Day. It's been a long time, hasn't it?"

"Not long enough, you old sleaze," Day shot back, though she smiled when she said it. "How are things in the Economic Control Corps?" Dana McKinnon worked for a high tech consumer and corporate affairs investigation branch. They'd worked together in the past when their cases had overlapped.

A capsule appeared in McKinnon's hand and he gave it to her. "Sorry about the stunner," he said. "Here, take this." He got up. "I'll get you a glass of water to wash it down." McKinnon went into the other room and Day heard water running. He returned with a glass of water and handed it to her. She swallowed the pill and took a sip of water, then held onto the glass.

"So what's with the stunning?" she asked. "You guys moving toward milder recruiting tactics these days?"

McKinnon laughed. "No, we still steal orphans and brain-wipe them when we need operatives." He took her hand, helped her to her feet, and led her over to the couch. He motioned to her to sit down. McKinnon sat next to her. "Besides, we don't raid other organizations. We leave that type of thing to your Auntie, and I understand she's thinking about doing just that. By the way, how is the old bag?"

"Same as always, the last time I saw her. Well, didn't see her. You know what I mean, you never actually see her."

"Makes her real credible, eh?"

Day shook her head. "You'd have to be there to understand. I don't know how much of her is showbiz or why she won't let us see her, but once you meet her you're convinced she's straight. Not that you have much choice but to believe her. Anyway, she's fine, and as much fun as ever. And, you still haven't told me what was with the stunning. And it had better be good."

McKinnon stood up. "It's good. Auntie got a hold of my bosses and asked us to offer you any assistance we could."

"Some assistance," Day said. "At least she got my report. But that's no reason to jump me."

"Aw, c'mon, Supra 9," McKinnon said. "You know damn well if my people had just shown up and asked you politely to come with them you would never have done it. You know what you're like." McKinnon looked at Day with a funny expression on his face, sort of a mixture of respect and curiosity. "Besides, your Club told us about the little episode there at New Las Vegas, at your hotel. That was pretty nice work, that escape."

Day smiled again. "For all the good it did me." She brought

McKinnon up to date with her retirement, and its subsequent blowing up in her face. He whistled appreciatively and his eyes grew wider. "So that still doesn't explain the stunning" she concluded.. Why didn't you meet me yourself? I would have come with you."

McKinnon shook his head. "Couldn't get away. And I knew you'd never trust a note from me or anything like that. You're a suspicious lady, Bonnie. But don't change! So I had to call in reinforcements." He shrugged. "Sorry."

"Forget it. I do tend to rely on my own devices a bit more than some people think is wise. But it's kept my hide in one piece this long..."

"True. Well anyway, you're here now. Mind if I let my people come in and apologize in person? I told them to be as gentle as possible, but I gather you were trying to run off in your patented manner."

"Yeah, that old self preservation thing."

McKinnon leaned over the coffee table and touched a spot on it. "Griff and Tehkt, you can come in now." He turned back to Bonnie. "They're really pretty good operatives, though they've got a way to go before they're in our league."

Day snorted "In *my* league, don't you mean?" Before McKinnon could reply, the door slid open and the four-armed alien who had stunned Day came in, followed by a reptilian creature Day recognized from Dolchworld. They bowed rather gracelessly.

"Our humblest apologies to you, Miss Day," Fourarms said in its thin, reedy voice. It crossed its arms behind its back and stood up straight and tall, proud as punch of its coup over the great Bonnie Day.

"Please accept my regrets, too," the lizard, Tehkt, said.

Day looked him up and down. "I didn't see you there," she remarked. "Where were you, sunning yourself on a rock?"

Tehkt's smile disappeared, but it remained standing proudly. "I was nearby. Griff is very swift and smart, but not strong. I was needed to carry you here."

"All brawn, huh?"

"You could say that if you wish," replied Tehkt stiffly.

"But it wouldn't be fair," McKinnon added quickly. Then, to his compatriots, "Thanks."

"No hard feelings, fellows," Day said cheerily. "A large headache, perhaps, but no hard feelings." Griff and Tehkt turned and left the room. Day caught a glimpse of an office outside before the door slid shut behind them. That shot down her theory about being in a hotel. "Where the hell am I, Dana?"

"As you've probably guessed, you are occupying the VIP Guest Suite of our Scree DiPont office."

Day stood up and paced the room. "Fine. So what assistance are you so generously offering?"

"I don't know what you need, but whatever we can do we will."

Day outlined her plan of action to McKinnon. He nodded. "Sounds logical to me. What can we do?"

"What do you know about Stornoway?"

"Everything. Unfortunately, there's nothing to tell you. Just your average big manufacturing company. Private enterprise at its height. You need help busting in?"

"I'm not going to bust in. I'm going to walk in the front door and talk to them."

"You must be mellowing with age."

"Ouch. Say, there's one thing you can do for me. You could tell me where I can find a decent restaurant. You've been here for a while. You must be familiar with the place as a whole."

McKinnon nodded. "And that's exactly what it is, too." Day grimaced and threw a withering look at him. "I've never seen such a pit," he continued, "And I've got another year before I get a new assignment. As for a restaurant, I know just the place. Shall we?"

"I thought you'd never ask."

McKinnon took her to a very fine Chibahtan restaurant he knew. He bought her dinner and they ended the evening dancing until the wee hours in a small, dingy club in the "arty" section of town. When they'd closed the place, McKinnon escorted Day back to her hotel.

After a leisurely breakfast, McKinnon excused himself, explaining that he had to get back to work. Day thanked him for the previous evening and kissed him good-bye at the doorway. Then she showered and dressed, loading up with weapons, recorders, snoopers, her normal accoutrements. She checked herself in the mirror to make sure nothing untoward showed: a little cleavage could help, a blaster would hardly be subtle. She told the room's secretary to arrange an appointment with the Sales Manager of Stornoway and, after a suitable pause, the machine reported that she was confirmed for four o'clock. Day realized she'd better get a move on.

Driving a ground car during a Henning City mid morning was a crowded, noisy, and unpleasant experience. Day fed her destination into the Marshall's navoguide and the big car picked its way through streets congested by commuter cars, public transportation, and huge, dirty and noisy pieces of equipment. It seemed as if almost every route she took was under construction at some point, like most major cities. As much as Day had looked forward to grounding again, Scree DiPont, or at least Henning City, wasn't exactly what she'd had in mind.

There didn't seem to be any traffic laws, either, except that virtually every intersection had a traffic signal that stopped the flow in Day's direction. At least the Marshall was comfortable. She preferred the unapologetic luxury of the Xannyk, but a space yacht was hardly practical for threading through idiots in a crowded city center. Day never understood why some planets outlawed personal commuter air traffic, though judging by the way these Scree DiPontians drove, they were probably better off staying in two dimensions. She thought they should also have made the use of auto drivers mandatory because the natives were obviously convinced – falsely – that they could drive.

Then again, even auto drivers weren't perfect. "Idiot!" she yelled, rather uselessly, as a lumbering robot garbage collector swerved in front of her, cutting off the Marshall as it crossed to the other side of the street. She gave a rude gesture, then felt stupid for letting herself get rattled by a brainless drone machine that wouldn't even notice, let alone appreciate, the use of her particular hand movement. Finally, traffic started thinning as she neared the city limits, and in the near distance Day could make out the huge complex her navoguide informed her was the universal headquarters of Stornoway Industries. She would have guessed it anyway: surface and space craft in various stages of construction were plainly visible and huge, hangar-like buildings spread their immense bulks over the land like a collection of some giant child's toy building blocks.

Compared with the city, the Stornoway complex was squeaky clean. Buildings and ships alike gleamed, as much as they could in the hazy, polluted daylight and, as Day watched, a drone maintenance ship appeared from behind one building and lumbered over to clean the hull of a gigantic freighter. It sprayed it with a fine mist of something, rinsed it clean with a different spray, and moved on to the next ship. No scrubbing seemed necessary. Day could smell a stollar in that cleansing solution; what a great consumer item! She could think of several places in the Co-operative where the stuff would sell like hotcakes. She'd start with that hotel in which she was staying...

She put the Marshall on manual and brought it to a halt outside the huge mesh gates. Presently, a small robot rolled out of the complex and came over to the vehicle. Day opened the Marshall's side window and leaned outside.

"Hello. What can I do for you today?" the robot asked politely as it reached the car.

"I'm Bonnie Day," she replied. "I have an appointment with your Mister Kerr at four o'clock."

There was a whirring noise as the machine mulled over what it had heard. "Very well," it said. "You are ten minutes early, but that's okay. Follow the bouncing ball through the gate and it will lead you to a parking stall. From there go into the first door you see and check in with the receptionist."

"Thanks," Day said sweetly.

"You're welcome. Have a pleasant day." The robot backed away from the Marshall. A metal ball about half a meter across detached from somewhere on it as the gate started swinging open; it rolled through the opening, hopping along with an ungainly, swaggering gait like a drunken spacer. Day eased the car forward behind it. The "bouncing ball" led her past several assembly buildings and Day could see many more ships-in-progress inside them. Stornoway seemed to be doing a booming business. Day was fascinated by the many diverse models of carrier that were being built at the facility.

Finally, the ball bounced through a space between two ground cars and began hopping on the spot on the sidewalk beyond. Day took that as her cue to park, and guided the sedan into the indicated stall. She was in a space barely large enough for the big vehicle, hemmed in by ground cars on either side. When she shut down the Marshall the ball hopped away and returned in the direction from which they had come. Day got out of the car and looked around. Directly in front of her was a map of the complex, conveniently placed for visitors. A large "X" on it bore the caption "YOU ARE HERE." The "first door," as the robot at the entrance had advised her, was a few meters from where she stood, mounted into a building with a sign saying "General Sales Office." She walked over to it and went inside.

"Please have a seat, Miss Day," a voice from an unseen person said. It sounded friendly enough, in a professional way. Day was in a small reception area filled with the humming of secretarial equipment. She went over to the row of four chairs and sat on one. "Thank you," the voice went on. "Mister Kerr will be with you momentarily."

"Thanks," Day replied. She looked around, saw some magazine pads on a table beside the chairs, and picked one up. She turned it on and started flipping through the menu. There was a broad range of trade publications, and Day called up one devoted to the latest in luxury yachts. She was just getting interested in a pictorial on the new Chimbaccis, which were rumored to be giving Xannyks a run for their money, when the door at the other end of the room opened and a tall man strode in, hand extended in welcome.

"Miss Day," he boomed. "Welcome to Stornoway Industries! I'm

Jeffrey Kerr. I hope I haven't kept you waiting too long?"

Day smiled demurely and extended her hand. She remained seated. "Not at all," she said as Kerr grabbed her dangling appendage and shook it. "Pleased to meet you, Mister Kerr." She flipped off the magazine pad, lay it on the chair next to her. "In fact, I was just getting interested in an article here."

Kerr beamed the salesman's beam. "Something about one of our products, I hope?"

"Not exactly. I was reading about the new Chimbaccis."

"Ah, yes, lovely machines. But they have no history."

"Not yet," Day agreed, "But if they keep building 'em like they have been it won't take long before they knock a few complacent manufacturers off their pedestals."

"Hmm. Perhaps. Well, why don't we go to my office. It's much more comfortable. Then we can discuss our business." He offered Day his hand once more and helped her to her feet. They went through the door and down a long, richly appointed corridor, Kerr extolling the virtues of the Stornoway operation as they went, passing by a variety of holos showing various models and corporate highlights. He outlined the company's history, philosophy, and products while Day pretended to be properly impressed.

They reached Kerr's office and went in. It was large and lush, as befitted his position in the corporate hierarchy. Kerr held out a chair for Day and she sat down. He went to the other side of his large, leatherish-covered desk and parked in his own chair.

"And now, Miss Day," he said when they were settled, "How can Stornoway help you?"

"I need a new yacht," she told him, "Something big enough to hold my family and myself and something I can throw big parties in and go on long trips."

"Interesting." Kerr picked a vapor pipe from his desktop, fired it up, and sat back smoking for a moment. "This is hardly the sort of product we normally deal in, though. Have you considered something like one of the larger Chimbaccis you were admiring earlier? Not that I want to recommend a competitor, mind you. Or, if you want to deal with a known quantity, there are the Xannyks, the Worsters, the Orions, any of a dozen excellent, high end products worthy of someone with tastes like yours."

Day shook her head. "No. I already have a Xannyk, top of the line. Not big enough, and it's starting to bore me." She leaned forward. "What I want is something big, and I was thinking the only thing to do would be to buy a cargo ship and have it converted." She unreeled the cover story she'd invented, the spoiled rich kid. Kerr leaned closer to her as she talked, his eyes growing larger and glowing brighter at the thought of the commission this woman was about to drop in his lap. Day prattled on, describing what amounted to a Class IV freighter like the one that had hit the QUEEN VICTORIA.

Kerr was scribbling madly on his desk pad as Day talked and when she finished her description he put down his stylus and looked up. "Well, I certainly can't accuse you of not knowing what you want! Of not thinking big, either. I can understand why you would come to us." He motioned to a chart on one wall. "This is a substantial order, and tailor made for our corporation. At Stornoway, we manufacturer more cargo vessels than any other company in the Co-operative and, if I may say so, our reputation is beyond reproach."

Day nodded, suppressing the desire to gag at the obvious pitch. "That's why I'm here" she said dryly.

"That's one hell of a yacht, if I may say so, Miss Day," he said in awe. "You've obviously thought this out very well and, from your portfolio, you can obviously afford such a project." He smiled at her, stollar signs dancing behind the pupils of his eyes. "You wouldn't by any chance want to adopt a son, would you?"

Day smiled right back, their eyes locked together. "No, thanks, I've had five of my own already. Three daughters, too. That's plenty for anyone."

"I must say, you don't look any worse for wear."

"Thanks. It's amazing what they can do, isn't it?"

"I hardly think anything you may have is fake or has been worked on," Kerr said appreciatively. "But back to business. We don't normally do special orders like this, but I'll tell you what we *can* do.

We can sell you a basic ship and contract out the refitting to meet your specifications. Would that be acceptable?"

She assured Kerr it would be more than acceptable. "But I'd like to check with some owners of the same type of ship," she said. "You know, people who've done the same sort of thing I'm looking to do. I want to see how it worked out for them."

"I can assure you they would have been happy with our service," Kerr said sharply.

"No, no. You don't understand. I'm not looking for a testimonial to Stornoway's service...I just want to see if they've got any ideas or recommendations that might help me design my ship. You know, pick their brains and see if there's anything they'd do differently, or do the same way only better."

Kerr unruffled his feathers. "Sorry. I may be able to help you there. As you may or may not know, we're required by law to keep ongoing records of all ships we build, so we should be able to pull the information from our databanks. That is, however, if the customers are willing to speak with you. Some may value their privacy. You know how people are sometimes..."

"Of course," Day said, ears perking up. "How long would such a search take?"

"We should have an answer for you by tomorrow morning. Is that soon enough?"

"Perfect. I must commend you on your service."

"It's a competitive industry, Miss Day. And we have no intention of giving up being number one."

Day stood up and grabbed Kerr's hand. She shook it. "Well, I guess that's all there is to discuss right now. I'll anticipate your call sometime tomorrow, then."

"Would you like me to walk you out?"

Day shook her head. "I can find my own way, thanks. I'm sure you're very busy. Thanks for your time." She walked to the door, which opened as she neared. Day went back outside and returned to the Marshall, pausing before getting in to look over the big sign with the map on it. She memorized it, then got into the vehicle and returned to her hotel.

The secretary's alarm woke her at one o'clock, digital. Day got up and went over to the dresser, where she'd arranged her inventory for the night. She slid into her Chameleon Suit, a Club issue costume, then loaded up its pockets and pouches with the equipment she'd deemed prudent earlier. It was time to go.

# SNEAKING A PEEK -- Chapter 9

Bonnie Day parked the Marshall in a public lot about a kilometer from Stornoway and covered the remaining distance on foot. Keeping to alleys and darkened deserted streets, Day covered the distance quickly.

She could see the complex's lights reflecting off the hazy cloud cover even before the plant itself came into sight. Using the glow as a guide, she made her way to where a street ended close to the huge factory. There she paused to get a good look. It wasn't as active as it had been during her earlier visit, which was the whole point of the early hour, though it was by no means deserted. She could see vehicles driving around the grounds and the low thrumming noise of the factory at work told her there was a night shift on duty.

As she watched, a robot sentry floated into sight, keeping its electronic eyes peeled at the plant's perimeter, as it searched for unauthorized visitors. Day sighed. All that activity was going to make things more difficult, though she was still confident she wouldn't have too much trouble getting by any obstacles she might find in her way. Since it was the night shift, Day assumed her target would be closed and locked; that suited her just fine. With luck she'd have uninterrupted access once she ran the gauntlet between the perimeter fence and the building itself.

Another sentry robot floated quietly along the fence. Day waited for it to pass out of sight, then hunched down and scurried across the empty space toward the fence. She noted with some satisfaction that her suit was working properly; it had assumed the color of the dirty pavement over which she was traveling.

She was ten meters shy of the fence when she heard the telltale hum of another sentry robot. She dove to the ground and froze, relying on her suit to do its job. Since Day's face was kissing the pavement she couldn't see the little sphere as it approached, but she could hear it through her hood. As had the others she'd seen, the sentry floated along some five meters inside the fence, scanning the perimeter of the plant with its beams.

There was nothing unusual about the sentry; it was a standard security model available almost anywhere. They were generally equipped for motion, heat, and weapons detection, and were armed with a high-powered stunner. They were quite reliable additions to a company's security section.

Unless, of course, the potential intruder was wearing a Chameleon Suit which, under most circumstances, was very unlikely. Besides their background-matching capability, Chameleon Suits, because of their dense material, were impervious to normal security scans.

The little sphere came closer to where Day lay sprawled, its low hum getting louder as it approached. She tried to lie even more still, if such a thing were possible. Slowly, she drew in a deep breath, then held it. The robot was exactly opposite her, on the other side of the fence, when it stopped. It hung in the air, searching the area outside, its sensor beams passing over Day's prone form several times before, apparently satisfied, it moved on again.

Day could hear it getting farther away and, as the distance between it and her increased, slowly let out her breath. When the machine finally passed from earshot she lifted her head and looked for it. It was gone from view, as she'd expected, but how long until the next nosy neighbor came along? She hadn't timed the spacing between the sentries, but figured it would only be a matter of moments until the next one poked its ugly dome into view by the fence. Time to get moving.

Day scrambled to her knees, checking for signs of movement inside the compound. It seemed safe, so she moved quietly toward the fence and stopped just short of touching it. Stornoway management was obviously security conscious, so the fence would be wired. She'd have to overcome the booby trap before she could get through and she'd better do it some place a little more sheltered than where she was. She looked along the fence to the left and right. There, about a hundred meters away was a gnarled tree that would provide some shelter. It would have given her a terrific perch from which to swing over the fence using the equipment she'd brought, too, but the possibility had been taken care of in advance. Someone, presumably working for Stornoway, had trimmed the tree's branches clear of the fence, doing a thorough enough job that there weren't any suitable limbs extending to overhang the fence.

Day shrugged. A quick hop over the fence, swinging from her "fishing line," would have been quicker and easier, but there was no point in worrying about it. At least the tree, and the little building on the other side of the fence from it, would keep her reasonably safe from the sensors of the sentries.

Then, as if on cue, she heard the telltale hum of another sentry robot approaching. She threw herself back onto the ground and froze. The hum got louder as the robot neared. Then, after another eternity, it faded in the distance. When it was quiet again Day peered out from under her hood.

All clear. Crouching low, she headed toward the tree. Twice more she froze before making the cover of the thick trunk, as the little sentries passed by her, one coming from each direction. Panting, she pulled herself into the comparative safety behind the tree and rested a moment while her Chameleon Suit changed appearance to match it.

After she caught her breath she reached into a pocket and pulled out what looked like an electrical device. Sticking her hand around the tree, she aimed its sensor at the fence and waved it through the air to take a reading. After a few seconds she brought it back and looked at its display. A simple electrical fence. Good! Stornoway must have put all its money into the robots, and any other surprises that might be waiting for her inside the compound, because the fence was about as old tech as they came. She'd have no trouble hot wiring it.

Another sentry floated into view and Day was once more forced to freeze. She wished someone would invent an invisibility screen that would mask movements as well as vision; then she could just ignore the annoying sentries. But it was ridiculous to pine for such a gadget, though she made a mental note to ask Jing how hard it would be to develop one. It would make a nice addition to her inventory.

When all was clear again, she put away the sensing unit and pulled out some hair-thin wire. She unreeled a length and cut it into four sections before she was forced to wait again for a sentry to float by. She hid the wire back inside the pouch, in case the metal would set off the sentry. It must have worked, because the robot went by as if nothing was wrong and in a moment passed from view.

Day moved around the tree and faced the fence. This would be the critical time when, except for the little shed on the other side of the fence, she would be in plain view of the sentries. She hated relying on the shed, and luck, for cover, but had little choice. It was either break through there or wait for someone to invent that invisibility screen, and she didn't have time to wait that long.

She pulled the hood down over her face, leaving only the eyeholes exposed. That should have been safe enough, at least theoretically. The eyeholes were cloaked with a one way surface that, to an outside viewer, would look the same as the rest of the suit. Unfortunately, that theory was capable of blowing up in one's face at the worst possible times, and she hoped it wasn't about to happen right then.

The fence was about two meters from the tree trunk, but just as Day was about to slink across another sentry floated into view. She froze and, rather uselessly, closed her eyes and waited for the sentry to pass. This would be the test. She had no place to hide, and no time to hit the dirt as she had before.

The robot floated along inside the fence, humming its low hum with no change or other indication that it thought something was amiss. It worked! As the sentry disappeared behind another building Day mentally thanked the techs who had designed the Chameleon Suit.

She stole a quick glance in the other direction, noted it was clear, and moved closer to the fence. She knelt down next to it and gave the metal strands a quick examination. She wouldn't have much trouble getting around this fence, she thought as she re-opened the suit's pouch and pulled out the strands of wire she'd cut. Vertical wires ran every half meter or so and all Day needed to do was connect her wire to a pair of them before she could safely cut the horizontal wire that linked them. Which is exactly what she did. She pulled some insulating tape from the pouch, wound it around the center section of each new fence wire, then taped them all together and attached the assembly to a horizontal wire higher on the fence. Twice during the procedure she had to freeze for sentry robots, but both instances went smoothly and no alarm was sounded.

Day was grateful for whoever at Stornoway had been sold on the idea of sentry robots for the perimeter. It could have been a lot worse if the company had spent its defense budget on an all-sensing fence, one equipped with infrared, motion and metal detectors. She'd have been in a great deal of trouble by then. This fence, which would only yell for help if the current through it was cut, was something she'd learned to get through by the time she was five years old.

Her handmade gate complete, all that remained was for Day to stoop down and go through it.

It wasn't quite time yet, though, because another of those annoying sentries was on its way. Day wished she could just blast the things and be done with it, but knew that would be one of the more stupid things she could do. Then it was gone and she was through the barrier. She paused and straightened her replacement wires, trying to put them back close to where the cut wires were. It wasn't a great job and was sure to be noticed by anyone who looked hard enough, but it resembled the original fence closely enough for casual glances. It would have to do. To hang around and fix the fence properly would take too long, and she needed to get away from the sentry robots which were slowing her down and increasing her chances of being discovered. Besides, it would make a great exit place as well.

By then it was about time for another visit from a wandering sphere, so she lunged forward and ducked around the side of the shed. She froze and waited while her Chameleon Suit's coloring caught up with her, then crept around to the front corner.

Her senses had been right. She heard the humming of a sentry approaching and, cursing the bother they caused her, turned to stone once again.

The sentry passed and Day stole a look around the shed, into the compound. There was a large open space she'd have to get across, about sixty meters by her estimation, to a pile of plastic cargo bins that was the closest cover. An easy sprint she could attempt between sentries. Beyond the cargo bins was a shadowy space a couple of meters wide and, behind that, the first major building rose.

The building for which Day was heading was a kilometer or more away, but once she was under the cover of the cargo bins she was confident the rest of the trip would be easy. It was obvious from noise of the complex, even though the sound of machines in production was admittedly muted compared with its daytime cacophony, that there was at least a partial crew working the night shift. There were also the rumbling and shrieking sounds of heavy machinery moving in the distance, noises that made Day glad she didn't work there.

She froze again when the inevitable sentry came along, then relaxed when it moved by and took a last look around. The coast was clear.

She ran, trying to be as light-footed as possible while making the best time she could. As far as she could tell she hadn't been noticed and in a few seconds, panting and catching her breath, she was in the darkness behind the cargo bins. It hadn't been a run that would have made her proud back in her track and field days, but it was okay for an old gal in her condition.

The Chameleon Suit was by then mimicking the shadow in which it found itself, making Day almost invisible as long as she remained behind the cargo bins. That suited her just fine, so she crept along behind the sheltering row until it ended just before the corner of a large building. And that was where her cover ended.

Day was forced to leave the shadows and cross the next several hundred meters slithering along the edge of the big, gray metal building. There were small items of cover, refuse dumpsters, incinerators, and the odd parked vehicle, but for the most part she was acutely aware that she would be a pretty good target for anyone who noticed her. As handy as it was, the Chameleon Suit couldn't keep up with the different grades of coloration on the big, dirty building as she sneaked along as quickly as she dared. She had never liked being a target. Not for the last time, Day cursed Auntie for dragging her back into the service.

She took small consolation in the fact that she hadn't seen any of those sentry robots for a few minutes. She assumed they were used strictly for perimeter duty, and as such they made a fine defense. After all, the average corporate spy or run of the mill thief would never have a Chameleon Suit, or Day's training and background.

The coast still looked clear, so she moved into the light and crossed over to the side of the next building, then paused to give her suit a chance to match its worn and dirty appearance as best as it could. After a few seconds, Day was creeping along the wall toward the next item of cover, a huge trash bin. She waited there long enough for another quick reconnaissance and blend-in, then pressed onward.

She made fairly good time and soon, by darting from cover to cover, she was at the end of the street and crouched behind a water truck. Still clear.

She stepped out and headed into an alley that ran at right angles to the street she had been on, then nearly jumped out of her skin thanks to a loud shriek followed by the roar of a machine starting up a short distance away. The noise increased, hoverjets squealed as they went to work fighting gravity, and whatever type of vehicle it was began moving. Day could tell from the increasing volume of the grinding and shrieking that it was moving in her direction.

She ran, then dove behind a parked vehicle on the opposite side of the alley. Blood pounded in her ears as she peeked around the rear of the vehicle and looked down the alley. Had she been seen?

Gaining speed as it lumbered toward her was a big garbage truck, its hoverjets whining and straining to keep it the requisite six inches from the pavement. Extended in front of it were two huge, metal claws at the end of long, jointed arms that would grab the trash containers and shake their contents into the hopper on its back.

The monstrous truck was dirty and probably didn't smell very good, either. It came careening down the alley toward her, lurching from one side to the other as it searched for dumpsters. Then it passed by in a rush of air, noise, and stench, and Day relaxed. "Whoever's driving that should have his head examined," she remarked under her breath. The truck ground to a halt at a stop sign, lurched around the corner into another roadway, and was gone.

Day looked around, then continued up the alley in the same direction as the truck. Halfway to the next corner, she crossed the alley and continued on the other side, where there were more shadows and she could make better time.

Ten minutes later she was standing across the large, open square from the building that housed Stornoway's data processing section. Aside from the subdued lighting and general lack of activity, it looked much as she remembered it from the map she'd memorized that afternoon. The door through which she'd entered faced her, and she could see another door farther along to her left.

She reached into her pouch and brought out a pair of snoopers. She fitted them over her eyes, letting the strap dangle instead of taking the time to extend it around her head. She thumbed the control to "magnify" and took a long look. The lettering on the main door said "Stornoway Industries -- Computer Center," which caused her to breathe a little easier.

The snoopers also showed that the door was secured with what appeared to be a garden variety thumbprint identity lock. Getting in should pose no problem. She gave the rest of the building a quick going over to make sure there'd be no surprises and when she was satisfied that everything was as it appeared to be, removed the snoopers from her eyes, folded them, and stowed them again.

Getting across the square only took a few moments, though there was one time when she was about two thirds of the way across where she was given a start and had to rely on her Chameleon Suit yet again. The door to the computer center opened suddenly and a middle aged human came out accompanied by a Gleezard of the same apparent age, though as usual it was hard to tell with a Gleezard. They were chatting about something in a language Day didn't understand. The human gestured to punctuate his side of the conversation, while the blue, furry alien shook its head from side to side in disagreement. As it turned out, the two were preoccupied enough that they probably wouldn't have noticed her in her Chameleon Suit anyway, unless she'd been jumping up and down and shouting at them, and they continued their discussion to the corner of the building and disappeared around it, their voices fading as they got farther away.

Day finished crossing the square. So far, so good.

She looked over the thumbprint lock and, satisfied that it was standard issue, pulled another little device from her pouch. She placed it over the thumbpad and pressed a hidden button on it. The gadget extended four little arms that grabbed on and held it in place on the door and a sensorpad the size of the thumbpad reached down and covered it. A few seconds later it beeped once and Day removed the gadget and stowed it away. Then she put her thumb onto the door lock and waited.

There was a click as the lock disengaged and Day removed her thumb from the pad, opened the door, and went inside. It looked as if the door had once been a fire exit: she was on a landing in a stairwell with flights extending up and down in front of her. A sign on the wall pointed downward to "Reception" so she took the steps down to another door and when she went through it she found herself in a typical greeting area and cloakroom.

Day crossed to a large directory on the wall and looked up the location of the main data storage area, which she discovered was on the fourth and lowest sublevel, in the bowels of the building. She turned away from the map, and went back through a door on the wall opposite to the one through which she'd just entered. A pair of elevator doors stood opposite each other and on a third wall was a door marked with a red "Exit-Stairs" sign illuminated above it. Day didn't relish the idea of running into the night watchers, so opted for the stairs rather than risk being caught helpless in an elevator.

She opened the door a few centimeters and peeked into the area beyond. It was clear. She opened the door all the way and went into the clean and well lit stairwell. Its white walls reflected the light with a glare that would have hurt her eyes if not for the Chameleon Suit's filters. The stairs themselves and the floor, however, were dull gray. There was a janitor's closet on the landing and when she reached it she tried opening it. It wasn't locked and a quick look inside showed Day there'd be plenty of room inside for her to hide, if need be. She closed the door again and continued down the stairs. At each sublevel there was a thumbprint panel on the wall beside the door, though there were no locks on the doors themselves. Day figured they were check-in stations for the night watchers.

She reached sublevel four and opened the door a crack. Beyond were the elevators, backed by a large open space that was obviously the computer section. It featured hundreds of identical terminals arranged in rows that stretched right to the far wall. The place appeared dead except for a variety of patterns swirling on computer screens.

Day opened the door and went through, past the elevators and into the large room. She took a more leisurely inventory of the place and singled out a terminal in the corner farthest from the entrance to do her work, her theory being that it would offer her the best chance of cover if someone happened to stop by. She made her way over to it, pulled out the chair that accompanied it, and sat down.

It was ancient equipment. The terminal didn't even have basic multilingual voice input capability, and she positively chuckled at the sight of a keyboard, something she hadn't seen since dinosaurs had roamed space. Day thought it must have taken a contortionist, or a multi-tentacled species, to get up any kind of speed on the thing. The ubiquitous thumbpad identification verifier was mounted on the desk beside the terminal.

The central computer should have had her prints on file already, thanks to her picking of the outside lock. Day didn't want to take any chances, though. She pulled out her little lock picker and placed it over the thumbpad, where it went to work and, shortly, beeped that the job was done. She removed the tool and stowed it, then took out the wristcom and plunked it down on the desk beside the terminal. Day placed her thumb onto the identifier and waited for it to accept her print.

It only took a second. The monitor lit up in front of her, displaying a main menu that offered access to the various file sections. She hooked the wristcom into the terminal's external data transfer and told it to download everything it could find.

"I'm happy to take care of all that for you," the wristcom offered cheerfully. "But I can do better. I can download only the information that you want. Okay?" She shushed the computer into silence, grateful that at least the little device hadn't started arguing with her, or second guessing her, for a change. She whispered an order for it to digest all the historical data on Class IV freighters, and quickly. The wristcom beeped once and a light on it illuminated, indicating that the data was flowing.

Day leaned back in the chair and waited for the transfer to finish. For the moment, there was nothing for her to do except keep an eye out for night watchers. So far she hadn't seen any sign of them. But of course that only meant they were that much closer to showing up...

After a while the wristcom said "Transfer complete. Would you like me to search any other records?" Day told it no, then ordered it to make a backup into non-volatile memory, park and shut down. The wristcom complied. Day detached it from the main computer system and stowed it away again. All that remained was to get the hell out of there which, except for the perimeter sentries and Murphy's Law, shouldn't pose too much of a problem.

She shut down the terminal and the screen went dark. She stood up, pushed the chair back to where she had found it, straightened the Chameleon Suit and turned to leave.

"Just what the hell do you think you're doing?" a surly male voice barked rather than asked. Day jumped about a meter in the air and as she landed turned to look at the source of the intrusion.

A white-suited man stood by the elevators, the stairwell door closing with a soft click behind him. Whoever it was, he looked like he meant business. A low-powered personal blaster, the type many citizens carried for self defense, stuck out of his hand and pointed directly at Day's chest.

"Now," he ordered, "move into the light. Slow."

# ON THE RUN -- Chapter 10

Day held up her hands to show she was unarmed. She came out of the shadows and moved toward the man. He kept his eyes on her, making sure she wasn't about to pull a fast one.

Day looked over the man closely. He didn't look like custodial or night watch staff. He was pale complexioned, wore funny, wire rimmed glasses of a type she hadn't seen anywhere except in history books, and he had a thin goatee. It seemed to Day he looked like a throwback. Then she placed him: he had left the building earlier with that alien as she had crossed the square. Whoever he was, he was obviously in control of the situation and Day didn't like that one bit. Her eyes bored into the man as she took his measure, while simultaneously figuring the distance between them and coming up with a quick, emergency Plan "B."

His gaze never wavered, though by the look in his eyes Day could tell he was out of his element, that while he kept a gun handy he had never expected to use one. Still, such a person can be extremely lethal, and the lack of professionalism on his part in some ways made him more dangerous. While Day outclassed her opponent in skill and finesse, he had the advantage of raw, animal instincts and fear. There was also the fact that he was the one holding the gun.

She smiled, a broad, harmless gesture that usually warmed the hearts of men everywhere, little lines crinkling beside her eyes, further adding to the disarming effect. She'd have to brazen it out.

"Hello," she said innocently. "Why are you holding a gun on me?"

The man's gaze never moved. "Who are you and what are you

doing here?"

Bonnie's smile didn't waver, either. "I'm Rebecca Farm," she said, pulling a name at random from the collection she'd used over the years. It was a joke name culled from some ancient story, but it was believable enough. She shrugged. "Umm, I'm new here and I came in late to work on the terminals. You know, these things are dinosaurs and I wanted to get used to them on my own time, so I wouldn't get behind in my work." It was a load of hoohah, of course, and she knew it, but why not try?

"That's a load of hoohah and you know it," he said, gesturing with the blaster. "There's no one new here. I'd know, I'm the supervisor."

"You mean they didn't tell you?" Bonnie's eyes got rounder. "You're kidding! But I started today."

"Yeah? Then why didn't I see you here today?" It wasn't going well. The man wasn't budging, though she could plainly tell he'd rather get the uncomfortable moment over with. His finger twitched on the firing button.

"I was filling out forms, orientation, you know. All the song and dance new employees have to go through." She stopped smiling. "Is there something wrong?" She could tell he was beginning to waver. He looked confused, as if he half believed Day's story even though he knew the odds were against it about a hundred to one, and despite the inconvenient fact of her standing in front of him, wearing a magic suit he would never have seen before.

Then the moment passed and his grip on the blaster stiffened as his resolve returned. "Just don't move. I'm going to call Security." Without taking his eyes from her or lowering the weapon, he moved to a workstation and picked up a phone. For a split second he turned his eyes to the phone controls as he punched in a code.

It was all the opening Day needed. She was on him in a flash, bringing her hand down and chopping the hand holding the blaster. It clattered to the floor. Her other hand closed around the man's throat, fingers tightening as she pushed him away from the phone. He whirled around, eyes bulging from the shock and the pressure of

Day's fingers. His body slammed against the desk. He tried to cry in pain, but only got out a strangled "ARGAAATHHH" before Day's grip tightened and even that utterance was cut off. He went down, smashing the phone's handset against the hard floor. It splintered.

Day slammed her free hand into his stomach, letting go of the grip on his throat. He went something like "Mupphhhh!" and quivered once, then lay still. Day got off him and stood looking down at the body. He was out cold. He hadn't been much of a fighter, and it was just as well. He'd hurt plenty, too, especially his throat, when he woke up, but he wouldn't be permanently damaged. Day preferred that to killing him outright; it was sufficient for him to sleep long enough for her to get away. After that it wouldn't matter.

She stooped and picked up his little blaster, shoved it into a pouch. Even a pop gun like that could come in handy. She could think of a few casinos in which it would be worth its weight in gold; even a couple of nightclubs.

Then the alarm sounded. A loud ringing started up, jangling harshly on Day's nerves, and a red light began flashing on the phone's base unit. Day didn't need a translation. She ran for the elevator lobby.

She pressed the up button on the wall between the doors then made for the stairwell. The Chameleon Suit's padded soles kept the noise from her headlong rush to a minimum, at least low enough for her to be aware of thumping footfalls from any pursuers wearing shoes. So far, so good. If she was lucky, the security guys would have to come from another building and she'd have time to escape, or at least find a decent hiding place.

Not that night. As she reached the first sublevel a door clanged open a flight below and she heard pounding footsteps and the shouting of at least two voices. She reached the ground floor, but rather than leaving by a possibly-guarded door, she decided to keep going up to throw the posse off the scent.

She was in pretty good shape, and had the advantage of a healthy flow of adrenalin; the people chasing her did not close the distance between them. Then she reached the second floor, and the stairway ended. Barely slowing, she pulled open the door and ran through a set of offices, divided from each other by low, sound deadening walls. There were plenty of places to hide, but they were lousy; she'd be found in no time.

She ran over to the window, opened it and looked out. There was a ledge just below, wide enough for her to stand on. She had little choice. She squeezed through the opening and onto the ledge, facing the wall. She reached into the room and fumbled around until her fingers found and closed the blind, then she wriggled sideways along the ledge and away from the window. She heard the door from the stairwell open and the guards run into the room, puffing and out of breath. At least they made a lot of noise; she'd have no trouble keeping track of them...

Day stole a look downward. Below her was a sidewalk bordering the street that ran along the outside of the concrete square. A few shrubs dotted the edge of the building, but they'd hardly break her fall. She looked up. The roof was about two meters above her, and there was an overhang that would be hard to scramble over. She wished she'd thought to bring along that Martin flying harness Jing had.

A siren wailed, then two; whatever she did would have to be done in the next moment. She looked both directions along the ledge. She was only about fifty meters from one corner, and around it would be at least the partial cover of shadow. She went in that direction, moving one foot sideways, then the other, sliding along the narrow ledge.

The sirens got louder, coming at her from different directions. She kept moving toward the corner. She reached it and carefully stepped around, then was in the blessed darkness. She stopped, heart pounding. A security car screamed around a corner to her left, speeding toward the building, siren hollering and lights flashing. "I'm glad it doesn't have a searchlight," she muttered. The car reached the corner she'd just turned and slowed with a screech, jerking to a stop somewhere on the side of the building Day had just left. As its siren began to wind down Day heard the slamming of doors and the scrambling of feet. The second siren sounded as if it had reached the same street, and whatever vehicle it heralded also stopped on that side of the building. Day guessed from the noise they made that the people had gone into the building to chase her down. It gave her a few seconds in which to act.

She reached into a pouch, felt around inside. With a quiet curse she withdrew her hand and tried another pouch. Pay dirt! She pulled out a small reel of fine thread, held the reel to the wall and pressed a button on it. There was a small flash and the reel was bonded to the surface. Day unspooled some thread and strung it around her waist. She tied a good, strong knot, made a slight adjustment to the reel's mechanism and leapt. She fell freely, then slowed rapidly as the safety mechanism put on the brakes, and touched down with scarcely more thump than she'd get from jumping off a footstool. She untied the thread from her waist and blended into the shadows.

It was pointless trying to sneak out of the compound now that it had been put on the alert. Besides, once she reached the street there would be no shadows to hide her. Better to just brazen it out and make a dash for it. She pulled out her blaster and checked its charge; it would be adequate unless she ran into a small war.

She left the shadows and ran to the end of the building and across the street on which the security cars were parked. Despite the padding of the suit, her feet pounded against the hard surface of the roadway. Behind her, from a pair of guards standing sentry at the computer center door, there came shouts and as she ran across the square a blaster bolt slammed into the ground near her. She started zigzagging. Another blast hit near her and she could hear the sound of a car starting up just as a third beam struck nearby. The car screeched away toward the corner as it tried to get around the square and head her off on the other side. Yet another blaster beam struck near her.

She stole a look behind. They were chasing her on foot, too. She ran faster, panting. She would have run even faster if she had seen the rest of the security guards pouring from the building and running after her, but her attention was concentrated on the route ahead.

Then she was across the square sprinting headlong up the street in the general direction of the perimeter fence. The security car screamed around the corner and came toward her as if to run her down. Day heard the second car squeal away in the distance and knew she'd never make it on foot – and since her pursuers were using blasters against her, she was in a fight or die situation.

She stopped, panting desperately, and turned to face the car careening toward her. When it got to within fifty meters she raised her blaster, twisted the control to maximum, and took aim. Her beam hit the driver's side of the windshield. It disappeared and the car went out of control. Without a hand to guide it, the vehicle's motor whined down and the car came to a stop a few meters from her. A blaster bolt hit it from behind and the rear windshield was vaporized in a flash.

Day ran over to the car and crouched in its shelter. More beams stabbed at her, a couple tearing more pieces from the car. She peeked carefully over the fender and was unsurprised to see the second security car fly around the corner and turn in her direction. It caught up with, and passed, the guards who ran after her on foot. Day could hear more sirens in the distance and as she watched armed personnel spilled out of various alleyways, all appearing to head directly for the source of the hubbub.

It seemed to the source of the hubbub as if the population of the entire planet was trying to get her. She didn't have time to count the people, but the odds weren't in her favor. She pulled open the passenger door of the security car and climbed in. The driver was sprawled in his seat, his head almost separated from his body, his chin resting on his shoulder at a wild angle. There was blood all over his front. It dripped onto the seat and ran onto the floor. The sight would have revolted Day if she'd had time to think about it.

She pushed open the driver's door and shoved the body into the street. She got behind the controls and, keeping her head down, stomped on the starter. The car rose on its hoverjets. She eased it forward and turned it in the direction of the perimeter.

She gunned the throttle and was shoved backwards into the seat as the car leapt forward. She kept her head down as much as possible, but had to peek over the control panel to see. There was a bang as a blaster bolt tore into the bodywork and the car shuddered sickeningly. Without looking back, Day goaded the car along as quickly as it would go, which wasn't nearly fast enough for her needs. Energy beams stabbed at her from behind. A hole was torn in one corner of the roof and Day looked up to see open air.

The sirens were getting louder and she noticed her vehicle was getting slower. She looked at the control panel. A red light on it was flashing. She swore. A blaster shot must have hit the coolant reservoir, because the car was losing the stuff at a great rate, the engine was overheating badly, and a pounding, grinding noise had started up under the hood.

Then the engine quit completely and the car wheezed to a stop, coming to rest some hundred meters short of the perimeter fence. Day got out the passenger side and crouched behind what little shelter the car still provided. The second car was getting very close, and someone was leaning out the passenger window, trying to take a bead on her with a blaster rifle. Day reached for her blaster.

It was still inside the car!

She crawled back in and grabbed the weapon, then aimed it at the onrushing car through the shattered rear window. She let loose a shot, but her angle was bad and it sliced harmlessly through the air before dissipating. She crawled back out of the vehicle and once again ducked beside it. The rifleman returned her fire and a corner of the car disappeared in a cloud of twisted plastic and plastiglass. Day fired again, aiming at the passenger's side of the windshield. A large hole appeared in it and the rifle clattered to the ground and was left behind. She fired again, this time at the driver.

The car began to slow, swerving wildly. It crashed headlong into a light pole three meters from where Day huddled, and exploded.

Through the smoke and flame, Day counted at least twenty men still pursuing her on foot and from the sirens that were getting louder with each second she knew it would only be a matter of seconds before reinforcements would arrive. She glanced at the fence. It was annoyingly far away, and there wasn't much she could do except run for it.

She fired several shots to keep her pursuers from getting too cocky, then took off toward the fence, zigzagging along, diving onto the ground periodically and rolling back onto her feet without losing more than a pace in the process. Seventy five meters to go.

Day didn't know what would happen once she passed the fence, whether the guards would follow her outside onto public property, or whether the cops would be there waiting for her. She didn't have time to worry about it. A shot hit the ground centimeters from her foot and the hole it blasted in the pavement threw up a cloud of shattered debris. Day stumbled and went down, scraping her knee painfully.

Groaning, she struggled back to her feet and lunged sideways as a bolt hit the ground where she'd just been. She limped along as quickly as she could.

Fifty meters to go. Then she noticed a sentry robot hovering ahead of her, just short of the barrier. Its stunner was pointed right at her, though she should still have been out of range. It wasn't out of hers, though. She did a shoulder roll, screaming with pain as her scraped knee bashed into the ground, and when she rolled back onto her feet she let loose a blast. It missed. She dove forward, then sideways, as energy bolts tore into the ground around her. She fired at the sentry again and it exploded into a shower of metal particles that would have made a fireworks manufacturer proud. She ran on.

Twenty five meters. She dived into another roll. She knew the guards were closing fast. It wasn't a pleasant feeling. Another sentry robot came into sight, leaving the area near the fence and heading directly at her. She managed to pick it out of the air with a single shot and it, too, blew up in a most impressive manner, showering debris in a large circle.

Fifteen meters! She was close enough to make out the individual wires of the fence, though she couldn't see the point through which she'd earlier crossed through. It didn't matter now anyway, and she had no time to worry about finesse. She fired the blaster and waved the weapon over an area of the fence directly ahead of her, opening a huge gash in it. It wasn't pretty but it would do, if she could only get there.

She rolled again, landing hard and painfully twisting her good knee. For an instant she wished she'd parked the Marshall closer to the plant and left the motor running. A blaster shot landing nearby sent her flying once more, and she bashed an elbow roughly onto the pavement when she hit and rolled. She screamed and dropped the blaster.

The pounding footsteps sounded as if they were right behind her. The noise from the security cars was harsh and ringing in her ears. She picked herself up, shook her head to clear it, and started running as well as she could. Then she was at the fence and ducking through the gash she'd made. She was outside!

Her escape wasn't complete yet, though. Beams kept stabbing at her from the other side of the fence, and the section behind her and the trees around her were torn to bits. Fire broke out on the tortured trees, sending flames and smoke skyward and, fortunately, helping add some camouflage and confusion to the scene.

Day kept running, ducking, and rolling, as she crossed the broad street outside the factory and headed for the nearest corner. The angry shouts were getting a little fainter; the guards must have been staying inside the fence. That wasn't as much consolation as she'd have liked, though, because they were still shooting at her.

Then she heard sirens approaching from different directions outside the plant and knew the police were on their way. She'd better find a hidey hole, and fast!

There was a loud blast from an electronic horn and a big sedan lumbered around the corner on its jets, heading directly for Day. She leapt sideways to avoid it, but it slowed and pulled to a stop beside her. A rear door swung open and she heard a voice yell for her to get in. She scrambled onto the back seat. Even before she was settled on the thickly upholstered bench, the sedan made a one hundred eighty degree turn and took off as fast as it could, heading in the direction of the city center.

From around a corner a couple of blocks ahead came a pair of police cars, sirens wailing and lights flashing. "Better shake these people," Day urged the driver, who was hidden behind a privacy screen. There was little she could do, so she strapped herself in and took inventory of her wounds. One knee was scraped, bloodied, and bruised, but she suspected it looked and felt worse than it really was. Her elbow wasn't bad at all; the rap she'd received had made it ring, but hadn't caused any serious damage. It hadn't even torn through the Chameleon suit. She'd gotten off easily.

The car zoomed around a corner and shot up a side street. Day was impressed with the driver's skill. She leaned forward and rapped on the plastiglass separating the two compartments. "I don't mean to jiggle your elbow while you're working..." she said.

"Then don't," replied the driver curtly, voice distorted by the audio circuit that allowed passengers to communicate with their chauffeurs. The big car swung around another corner and bolted down a deserted, though heavily littered, alleyway. Day could see lights approaching from behind, then a police car turned into the alley. It burned up the road in pursuit. The car took another corner, almost overloading the right hand hoverjets, then shot out into an open boulevard. Day looked behind; the police car was still there.

The driver spoke into a microphone on his wrist, though Day couldn't hear what he said. Then the vehicle slowed, and the driver turned to face Day, smiling broadly. "I figured we'd better keep an eye on you." It was Dana.

"Well, you're handier than the Space Marines," she said, smiling. "As long as they keep stunners out of your hands."

"My pleasure." Day relaxed. Dana would get them out of this. Hell, if he couldn't out drive them, he'd use his influence. He seemed intent on out-driving them, though, which suited Day. She had a low bureaucracy threshold at the best of times and this definitely wasn't the best of times.

McKinnon threw the car into a long curve, a police cruiser gaining on them. McKinnon gunned the engine once more as they came back onto a straight stretch and the cruiser fell back. "So how do you propose to lose the heat?" Day inquired sweetly. "Vanish into thin air?"

McKinnon shook his head, now concentrating intently on his driving. "Just relax and leave it to us," he managed to say before guiding the car onto an off ramp and speeding onto a different artery. The police cruiser stayed behind.

Day knew it would only be a matter of time before the cops set up a roadblock, but kept it to herself; McKinnon was bright enough to know that as well. They passed a slow moving vehicle on the right and McKinnon gave its driver a jaunty wave as they went by. The car pulled in behind them, taking a line down the center of the road. "That's Griff," McKinnon said, motioning with his head to indicate the slower vehicle. "He's a hotshot behind the wheel but now he's just playing road hog. Fun, huh?"

The police car came up behind Griff's vehicle, and its driver leaned on the horn. Griff moved left as if to make room, but when the police car eased right to pass Griff pulled in front of it, cutting it off. The cruiser tried the other side, and once more Griff blocked it.

"I can just imagine how Griff's improving those cops' morale," Day remarked dryly as McKinnon pushed the vehicle toward its limits. Finally, the limo slowed down and turned into a dark lane. "How's Griff going to get loose from the cops?" she asked.

"Don't worry about him. He just held them up long enough for us to get away. By now he's let them pass and gotten lost himself. Here we are."

'Here we are' turned out to be a storefront at the dead end of the lane. McKinnon said a few words into his microphone and the entire wall moved upward and out of the way. They drove through the opening and into a large, immaculately clean parking area. The wall closed behind them and McKinnon brought the car to a gentle stop at the opposite end of the garage. He shut off the engine and turned to Day, beaming from ear to ear. "Pretty slick piece of rescuing, eh?"

# ELBOW BENDING -- Chapter 11

Day leaned back in the lush seat, a wry grin on her face. "Not bad," she said, "for a bunch of amateurs. Don't you think the cops are going to keep combing the area for you?"

McKinnon didn't return Day's smirk, and in fact looked a little hurt at her remark. But he said "Of course. Won't do 'em any good, though. Nope." He opened his door. "Let's get going." He stepped out of the big car. "But you might want to slip into something a little more appropriate." He motioned to a bag on the seat beside her.

"You thought of everything. Thanks." She wriggled out of the tight skin, folded it neatly and placed it beside her on the back seat. She pulled more conventional clothes from the bag, delighted to discover they were her own, and dressed, stowing the wristcom in her purse. She didn't want to take any chances of losing it; the garage appeared safe, and probably was, but she'd rather rely on her own devices.

As garages went, it was clean and bright, and had room for many more vehicles than were actually present. The only other transports there at the time were a light hauler and a nondescript, stubby black sedan that would hardly have garnered a second glance in traffic. There was a workbench, loaded with tools and other arcane gadgets, along one wall, and a door was in the wall opposite the entrance.

"Did I detect a note of complaint in your tone?" Day asked McKinnon after she rejoined him. "I mean, are you mad that the Club sent me into your territory?"

"Not really," McKinnon told her. "Our job here is support and surveillance. We're more or less a corporate crime unit, as it were.

We keep an eye on things and take whatever action is deemed necessary." He shrugged. "It's when troubleshooters like you show up that we get a little excitement into our lives. Otherwise it's mostly pretty routine."

"So you don't feel like I've barged in and taken over?" She liked McKinnon and was grateful for his friendship, and his timely help. She didn't want him nursing a grudge. He shook his head. "Nah. Don't worry about it." He laughed and gave Day a conspiring look. "Tonight was the most fun I've had since I was posted to this black hole. You really had that plant going, didn't you?"

Day laughed. "I think I missed setting off one or two alarms. They were probably wired badly." She grabbed McKinnon and gave him a big hug. "That's for picking me up. As you said, it was a pretty slick piece of rescuing."

"Our bill will be at your hotel in the morning."

"I always knew you were a mercenary at heart."

McKinnon smiled merrily with his eyes, though his mouth pouted. Just then, the entrance swung up again and Griff's vehicle came in. It moved at an unhurried pace that indicated he must have shaken off the pursuit. He parked and turned off the vehicle, the engine whining down to silence as the vehicle settled onto the concrete floor.

Griff got out smiling. "Boy, those cops sure cain't drive!" he said.

"I guess I owe you a beer, too," Day said as Griff closed the car door. He joined them and McKinnon and Day patted him on the shoulder.

His double pair of arms fluttered in an embarrassed gesture at the show of affection. "No problem, Miz Day," he replied wheezily. "I ain't driven like dat in months. It keeps me young!" He smiled and patted her shoulder in return, one arm doing the job while the other three stayed out of the way behind his back.

Day reeled at the blows, and he stopped. "Sorry, Miz."

"Hey, after pulling my hide out of the tanner you can poke my shoulder anytime."

McKinnon suggested a nightcap would be in order, an idea with which both Day and Griff heartily agreed. "Good," he said, "Because right next door there just happens to be a wonderful watering hole that serves the best booze from the top hundred worlds."

"How convenient," Day said.

"It's deliberate," Griff told her. "McKinnon put this hidey hole here cuzza the booze palace being there. The guy's a lush."

"That's why we love him," Day said. "Let's go. Drinks are on me."

"Well, here's to you and here's to me!" Day exclaimed, raising a glass of some smoking hooch into the air. "And to hell with the other S.O.B.!" Griff, whose beaker was filled with a foul-smelling brew, and McKinnon, who had a traditional beer, raised their glasses in response. The containers clinked together and the trio quaffed their respective poisons. A funny expression came over Griff's face as the liquid went past his taste buds, and he gave a mighty shudder as he swallowed.

"Smooth stuff, huh, Griff?" McKinnon said, laughing. Griff coughed once and nodded in agreement. "Hair of the mutated dog," McKinnon confided to Day. He chugalugged his beer, wiped the foam from his beard, and looked around for the waiter robot, waving his empty stein through the air. "Hey! Service!"

"Don't mind him," Griff said to Bonnie. "He's always a jerk when he drinks in public."

"I know," Day said. "It's not just when he drinks in public. His reputation is sparkling all through the Co-operative. No one wants to party with him anymore." McKinnon shot her a pained look and put the stein back on the table. He sat there quietly. "So tell me, fellows," Day said, "What made you show up at just the right time? I couldn't have asked for anything better than that if I'd been writing a holomovie."

McKinnon leaned back on the rear legs of his chair, tilting the seat into a rather precarious position. "Well, like we told you before," he said, "Your Auntie asked us to keep an eye on you and that's what we've been doing." He launched into a explanation of their version of the evening, that they'd tailed her to the plant in Griff's car, then cut himself off abruptly as the waiter robot showed up. Day ordered another round, two for McKinnon who, if history was any guide, would be determined to keep at least one drink up on the others, and the robot clattered away.

"You were saying?" Day prompted when the robot was out of mic shot.

"Yeah, well, we had a pretty good idea where you were going, because where the hell else would you be going?" Day gave him a look; McKinnon had never been one for oratory, but he always managed to get his point made no matter how strangely it came out. "We kept our distance so we wouldn't jiggle your elbow. After all, we're just here to help..."

"Do you miss field work?" Day interrupted.

"Me?" He shook his head. "Nope. You live longer my way."

"We'll see," Day said.

McKinnon did a double take. "Anyway, to continue my story," he stared hard at Day, who dropped her eyes and took a sip of her drink, "Griff dropped me off at your limo. Nice car, by the way. I must get one of them for myself."

"You should see my yacht!"

"Well, I'm jealous, but not enough to get back into the field. Much as I hate Scree DiPont, I'll take my hide without blaster burns, thank you."

"Anyway," Day reminded, "You were saying?"

"Oh yeah. Well, we split up to double our coverage and halve the chances of getting caught, if that's how the math works. I never was very good at math, despite being in this corps. Griff kept to his car, which is a lot faster than it looks. I sent Griff back to your hotel to pick up a change of clothes for you just in case and about ten seconds after he got back we heard all the alarms go off. Sloppy work there, Bonnie."

Day looked him straight in the eye. "Oh yeah? When was the last time you broke into anything?"

"Well, anyway, we gave you a few more minutes to make sure, and were heading in to pick you up when you ran out and saw me coming. The rest, as they say, is history." He looked pleased with himself.

The robot came back carrying drinks and placed them on the table in front of the trio. "Same tabs as before?" it said in a metallic voice that almost seemed to show a trace of boredom. Day told him to put everything on her bill and the robot clanked away.

"Well, the only question I have left is what to do with the Marshall. Can you guys cool it off for me?"

"Of course. We'll make sure it gets back to the agency for you. And it'll be clean. McKinnon downed the rest of his beer, then took a sip on the second one. "No, when that tank shows up back at the rental office it'll have new registration, serial number, the works. And their computers will recognize them. No one will ever know." He smiled, a few globs of suds hanging from his moustache. "When we take care of something, it's taken care of."

"How could I doubt you?" Day said. She reminded McKinnon of the Chameleon Suit, and inventory of ordnance, she'd left inside his car. McKinnon promised to have it delivered to her hotel room by morning. She relaxed. It was good to deal with competent people.

They tossed back a few more before calling it a night. McKinnon and Griff drove Day back to the hotel and she went up to her room and undressed. She was exhausted from the night's action, and for some reason the drinks hadn't helped perk her up, either.

She still had to review the data in the wristcom, but it could wait. The Xannyk's computer was faster, and less likely to be bugged, than the room's secretary. She went into the bathroom and, under the bright lights, looked at the wounds she'd received at the Stornoway plant. Ugly and relatively painful, but not serious. She took the medikit from the cabinet and gave herself treatment. Then she went into the bedroom, pulled down the covers, and fell into bed. She dialed up some soothing music and was asleep almost immediately.

Day woke up, got up, and went into the bathroom to take care of the business of refreshing herself. While showering she took another look at her wounds and was pleased to note they were already showing signs of proper healing. When she was scrubbed and glistening clean, she allowed the machinery to dry her and comb her hair. With a hearty breakfast, she'd be ready to take on the galaxy once more.

She went into the living room and ordered breakfast from room service and while waiting for it to arrive turned on the video to catch up on the news. Her escapade of the previous evening was all over it, with great footage of the wrecked security vehicles and ambulances taking away the casualties. The reporter was milking the theory that some suspected band of industrial spies was being blamed for the attack on one of the planet's leading corporate citizens, and that the perpetrators were still at large. The item ended with a comment from the Henning Police Force saying that it was only a matter of time before they had the criminals in custody.

Day smiled. She mentally thanked McKinnon and Griff again for their help and flipped off the broadcast.

The breakfast, along with a package from McKinnon, arrived as she was getting dressed. She told the dumbwaiter to put it on the coffee table, which it did before leaving. Day finished dressing then, as she opened the bundle from McKinnon, devoured the meal.

Breakfast finished, she retrieved the wristcom and sat it on the secretary. If that sales manager from Stornoway, Kerr, was true to his word, he'd be calling soon and she wanted to store his data in the little computer, too.

"Incoming call for you, ma'am," the secretary announced presently. Day moved over to the desk-like machine and sat down in its chair.

"Go ahead," she said. The screen lit with the image of Jeffrey Kerr. The sales manager looked harried, as if his day wasn't going well so far. Day wasn't surprised. "Hello?" she said sweetly.

"Good morning, Miss Day," Kerr replied. "Sorry I didn't get back to you earlier this morning. We, er, have been a little busy this morning." He looked directly into her eyes, though Day couldn't tell if the gaze had any particular significance to it or if he just knew how to use a pickup camera properly.

Day smiled again, her disarming look. "I'm sorry to hear that. I hope you get your head above water soon."

"Precisely. Anyway, nothing for you to be concerned with. But I have that information you requested."

"That's wonderful," Day replied, her poker face activated. "I compliment you on your excellent service."

"It is our pleasure. Do you have downloading capability?"

"Of course. "

Kerr permitted himself a small smile. "Excellent." Day could see him reach to his desktop. "Data transmission is underway. You can receive whenever you like." Day started recording; a light illuminated beside the screen, indicating the transfer had begun. "I can give you an overview while the computers talk."

Day nodded. "Good."

"There are several dozen good, used Class IV freighters on the market right now. Unfortunately, our information shows that the best of them are located inconveniently at the other end of the Cooperative. Oh, and the owners seem to be asking hefty prices, too."

"Too much?"

"In my opinion. Class IV's generally have a good resale value, but for what they're asking, considering the costs of getting there to inspect them, bringing them to a conversion company, and getting the work done and certified, you'd be better off buying, shall we say, a less than pristine example and having it completely stripped down and restored to your specifications."

Day pursed her lips. "That may make sense."

Kerr continued. "And there's another choice, since you're already here and, as you know, your credit is beyond reproach. You could purchase one of our freighters, raw, and take it to the converters. Which I believe was your first option when we spoke yesterday. It wouldn't cost much more, because you'd be buying a bare bones model and not a fully equipped Class IV like the ones that are presently on the market used. There's a lot of expensive equipment in them that is specific to industry and wouldn't be necessary in a personal ship like yours." He coughed a little "ahem."

"And you'd be getting full warranty. We are quite flexible."

"Go on."

"That's about the size of it. The specifics should be in your computer by now." As if to punctuate his remark, a gentle "beep" told Day the download was complete. She terminated the data link.

"It sounds like you've covered all the bases for me," she said. "Except I find it hard to believe that you'd have a brand new Class IV freighter I could buy off the rack. Don't you only make those things once the contract's signed?"

"Well, yes, but we do happen to have one unit that's basically finished and ready for outfitting. It would be perfect for your needs. Mechanically it's ready, but it's bare inside. You could have it outfitted however you'd like."

"How come it's not already spoken for?"

"Well," Kerr looked embarrassed, "Technically it is. It's being built for one of the freight lines operating in the rim planets. Part of an order for fifty ships."

"Doesn't that stink a little?"

"Well, technically, again. But they're a little slow on the bill, and it serves our purpose to redirect one freighter to you."

"That doesn't sound quite fair to me." As if it bothered her.

"The customer won't care, because they're experiencing what they called a slight cash flow problem right now. They'd be just as happy not getting the ship right now." He gave her an earnest smile. "So you'd actually be helping them, and us, by taking an extra freighter off our hands. Shall we write it up this afternoon? I would be most happy to meet you."

The guy knew how to close the sale, Day gave him that. "Okay, you're in the running," she told him, "But I'd still like to check out a conversion company to see if they can do what I want. And I want to look over some of the used ones. How long does it take to get a new one built from scratch?"

"Generally, a standard year, from first interest to final delivery, though as you can see we can sometimes find ways to take a shortcut."

"Okay. Even a year's not too bad. It's not as if my Xannyk is a rust bucket." She leaned closer to the video pickup. "Tell you what. I'll check out some of the alternatives you've given me and get back to you within a month. Don't worry about that ship you've got right now; I'm not quite ready and I don't want to keep you twisting in the wind."

"That's very thoughtful of you, Miss Day," Kerr replied, "Though not necessary."

She shook her head. "Don't worry about it. So who are these converters you recommend?"

"The one I recommend the most highly is a company called 'Littman Custom Conversions,' on Panadar. We often recommend them because they do excellent work and we've dealt with them for many years. They're warranty approved, too."

Day smiled knowingly. "And because you get a little thank you, right?"

Kerr lowered his eyes. "Well, friends do tend to show their gratitude, though it's by no means something that will let young Mister Stornoway retire early. Besides, I wouldn't recommend them if they weren't the best."

"I'm sure you wouldn't." She smiled. "Tell you what. I'll get back in touch with you as soon as possible and let you know what I've decided. Okay?" A gentle kiss-off. She'd used far more forceful ones in the past, on salespeople who had been less concerned with her needs than with their commission checks.

"That's fine, Miss Day. I hope we can do business. Yours may be a small order, but that doesn't make it any less important. We'll do our best to see that you pay as little as possible, too, when the time comes."

"I commend you for your attitude," she said, "and look forward to dealing with you soon. Thanks for everything." She switched off the link before Kerr had a chance to ooze another platitude her way and, as the screen went dark, booted up the wristcom and started loading the Stornoway data into it from the secretary.

Littman Custom Conversions seemed like the logical next stop; that black Class IV had definitely not been standard issue, and it would have had to have been overhauled somewhere. It was a place to start. The whole case smacked of a high-priced operation.

Panadar. That was about sixty light years away, two Jumps for the one way trip. That suited Day; she'd had enough of the filthy Scree DiPont and hoped she'd never have to return. She unplugged the wristcom from the secretary, told it to backup and park, and stowed it in her luggage. She looked at the clock. Four point six o'clock, time to think about moving on.

She reviewed what she'd found so far. Whoever had knocked over the QUEEN VICTORIA was well organized and well armed. They had bucks behind them. It could be a terrorist organization, which she thought the most likely, though it could also be a government with a vested interest in seeing that Ramallah and Bolingnar stayed at war. Or, it could be a wild card, and wasn't it always? That they were ruthless went without saying; the way so many innocent people had been killed aboard the QUEEN VICTORIA made Day think it was probably a fanatical terrorist group. Yet it didn't benefit anyone politically as far as she could tell. So who could it be?

She shrugged and got up from the secretary. She finished getting ready to leave, packing the rest of her things. She paused to tape a message for Dana McKinnon, and left instructions for the secretary to relay it to the message center for McKinnon's branch. Then she ordered a cab to take her to the spaceport, took a last look around to make sure she hadn't forgotten anything, and left the room. Checking out didn't take long and in a few minutes Day was sitting comfortably in the rear seat of a ground cab, being driven back to the Xannyk. She was grateful not to be driving; she'd had enough of Henning's traffic. After what seemed like an eternity, the cab pulled into the parking area at the spaceport. She paid the driver, got out, and went into the terminal building.

Five minutes later she was back inside the homey comfort of the Xannyk. She stepped out of her shoes and wriggled her toes in the thick carpet lining the floor of the bridge.

It was nice to be back.

# EXCURSION FOR CONVERSION
## -- Chapter 12

"Hello, Bonnie," said the yacht's computer, "I was beginning to think I'd been abandoned."

Day smiled. "What? I only left a couple of days ago."

"Yes, but that's an eternity in computer time. It was a joke. Did you like it?"

"Fine, fine." She looked around the bridge; all looked well. "Are you ready to leave?"

"Definitely," the computer said, and Day thought she could almost detect a note of satisfaction in the electronic voice. "I'm afraid this atmosphere may have done permanent damage to my hull."

Day laughed. "I somehow doubt it. It's probably nothing a good scrubbing wouldn't take care of at a nice detailing place."

"Am I correct in assuming we're not going anywhere near such a place?"

"Bang on, as usual. We're going to Panadar." Day tossed her bags onto the couch, then thought better of it and picked them up again. She took them back to her bedroom and tossed them on the bed instead, then started unpacking.

"Would they have detailing facilities?" the computer asked, hopefully.

"Perhaps," Day called out over her shoulder, rather unnecessarily since the computer could hear her no matter where she went inside the yacht, "But we won't be there long enough. If everything goes according to plan."

"Which means we may be there longer than you anticipate,

correct?"

"Do I detect a note of sarcasm?" From a computer, no less?

"Not at all, Bonnie, though I do understand how human schedules can somehow not amount to very much."

"You're right, of course." Especially in this line of work. Day finished unpacking and stored the bags. She went forward to the bridge and sat on the couch. "How about turning on the screen?"

The viewer lit up with an electronic window onto the scene outside. The pollution appeared particularly vile, casting a yellow haze over the field and smearing the view of the nearby city into a pastel-like image of a scene from a cheap viddy. "On second thought," she said. "Let's just get out of here. Kill the screen until we're in space."

The screen went dark.

"Departure Control signals all clear. Do you want an orbit or a straight out trajectory?"

"Let's get out of here." She ordered the Xannyk to head directly for the moon to pick up the shuttle they'd left there, then set a course for Panadar.

"Final checks complete. We're lifting from the pad," the computer said. There was no trace of acceleration or lift. "By the way, Bonnie," the machine piped up, "I believe I've computed a way to ensure the shuttle will stay attached during Jumps."

"I thought it wasn't a big problem."

"Not big, but an annoyance. But it won't be if we only keep the shuttle half the distance from us than we did with our last Jump, and use the towbeams to push it through the Jump ahead of us rather than pulling it behind us."

"That's it? Why didn't you think of that before?"

"I don't know. Perhaps I'm becoming obsolete."

Day laughed. "I doubt that's the case. Anyway, I'm glad you figured that out. We'll do it your way."

"Clearing the atmosphere."

"Such as it is," said Day. "And good riddance."

"I heartily agree," echoed the computer. "On course for shuttle pickup."

They retrieved the shuttle and set off for Panadar. True to the Xannyk's estimation, they completed both Jumps without incident and in eight days, subjective time, they popped back into normal space at the edge of Panadar's system, a double star with thirteen planets.

Day had spent most of the trip looking over the information she'd gotten. It was tedious reading, made even worse by the fact that nothing pointed anywhere specific. Half a dozen Class IV's had disappeared over the years. They weren't listed as destroyed, or scrapped, they merely no longer appeared in the files. That was odd, but there was nothing that gave any indication of what might have happened to them. Pirates, black market, who knew. Maybe someone had even absconded with one to use as a yacht.

Eventually, after she'd had the computer cross reference the service histories of all the Class IV freighters, she became convinced that she was on the right track, but a long way from the winner's circle. The Littman name had appeared over and over in the records, having apparently done a lot of work on many types of conversions, and for a wide range of clientele. Day was surprised to find that an aftermarket operator could be so big, so well known and so busy.

Poring over the Stornoway files depressed her. She'd almost been killed getting the information and all it told her for sure was that some ships were unaccounted for and Littman did a booming business! At least the records confirmed her suspicions that Panadar was where she should be heading.

Eventually, she saved and backed up the data and turned her attention to the task ahead. According to the Xannyk, Panadar was the fourth planet out from the larger, red star of the pair. It had a temperate climate, a stable government, and used Standard Cooperative time, so Day didn't have to worry about silly conversions. The planet was mostly water, with one huge continental mass straddling its equator, and it wasn't nearly as industrialized as Scree DiPont.

Littman Conversions was on the outskirts of the only major urban area, a mildly interesting place – according to the ship's commentary – called, without much imagination, Panadar City. The red primary gave the planet a dull crimson glow, even at the height of the day. It wasn't Day's favorite color for a sky, but it beat smog. The pictures showed that the rusty hue of Panadar's sky looked more bloodstained than breathtaking. She'd take deep green planets any day. Perhaps she'd retire to one. Hopefully soon.

As luck had it, Panadar had two moons and Day had the Xannyk head for the outermost one, so they could park the shuttle.

They left the little spacecraft in orbit and headed for the planet. The yacht entered traffic and began its controlled descent to the spaceport. It eventually kissed the ground softly at the berth assigned by Arrival Control and went automatically into its dirtside routine.

Day didn't need to bother with any of that, so she kept busy by flipping through slides of the various hotels in Panadar City before, disgusted, she decided to use the yacht as her base. Despite its small sleeping quarters, it offered a lot more amenities than she was likely to find in the city.

Her strategy for Panadar was to be a little more subtle than on Scree DiPont. She'd been sloppy there, or maybe she was rusty after her all-too-short retirement. She vowed to be more careful this time.

The Club's private records on Panadar listed all the places a Troubleshooter would be likely to find information for sale. These usually amounted to bars and nightclubs, the type of establishment frequented by petty thieves, informers, and other less-than-above-board creatures. The planet was small and unimportant, and normally very quiet, so there was no Club branch and even McKinnon's organization didn't operate there. Day noticed with interest that one of the places listed in the files was only a few blocks from Littman, so she decided to check it out first. It was a generic watering hole, according to the records, though it looked like it might have been a little tougher than many.

She closed the files and instructed the computer to make sure she had some Club issue identification before she left the yacht.

She got into a robocab on the city side of the building. "Destination, please," said the auto driver.

"Chuckie's, ninth level, street 469 East," she replied.

"Thank you. Computed. The fee is forty stollars."

Day fumbled in her purse until she found a fifty stollar note, fed it into the machine's money slot. It swallowed it without comment. "Don't I get any change?" she asked.

"Exact fare only," the cab replied and a sign Day hadn't noticed before lit up next to the slot, saying exactly the same thing. She sighed and sat back in the seat. The cab rose from the ground and headed for the city.

The trip to Chuckie's only took Day a few minutes, since Panadar didn't have any stupid rules against airborne commuter traffic. She was deposited outside the bar and the cab took off and headed back in the direction from which it had come. Day watched it soar off into the distance, then turned to examine Chuckie's.

It was actually quite nice, for a hangout. The facade was clean and bright, and ornate, lighted signs promised dining, dancing, games of chance, and exotic liquors. "Sounds like my kind of place," she muttered as she pushed open the front door and went inside. She paused in the foyer to let her eyes adjust to the smoky, dimly lit interior, then looked around. To her left was a cashier's station and an archway leading into the restaurant part. Ahead, a short corridor passed the washrooms and opened into the bar.

"May I help you?" asked a pretty human who had suddenly appeared behind the cash counter.

Day shook her head. "No thanks, I'm just going into the bar for a few minutes." The girl immediately lost interest.

"That's fine," she said, "Go straight on through. It's happy day today, drinks half price till midnight."

"Sounds good to me," Day replied. "Thank you." She went into the bar. Chuckie, or whoever ran the place, must have had a hush field installed, because as Day passed through the archway separating the corridor from the bar, she was hit by a cacophony of sounds. Bings, bongs, and boings from electronic games intermingled with loud, brash music and over it all was the rumble of many voices trying to be heard over the rest of the noise.

Day took in the sights and sounds. Ahead of her, stretched in front of the long wall, stood a huge wooden bar backed by the usual assortment of bottles, glasses, vials, pipes, and other implements of imbibing, inhaling, and intoxicating. To her left, on the short side, was a small casino area complete with flashing lights, bells, whistles, and the "ching, ching, ching," of payoff tokens falling into hoppers. Booths lined the other two walls, and a liberal sprinkling of tables made navigating one's way through the room a difficult prospect, especially for those who'd already been hard at work sampling the various poisons offered for sale.

A Spotted Menotroid got up from a table near where Day stood, its tentacles writhing randomly around it, and lurched drunkenly toward her. "Oudda my way," it said as it tried to squeeze by her. "Goin' to da liddle room." Day moved over to let the creature pass. It careened off a wall before finding the right door and disappeared into the bathroom.

Day threaded her way between the tables and went over to a vacant space at the bar. She hopped onto the stool and leaned on her elbows on the bar, squinting through the smoke at the other patrons lined up and down its length. It was a varied mix, and a rough-looking crowd indeed. Day was glad to be armed unobtrusively with her usual variety of ordnance. On her immediate right was a decidedly human patron, a towering man who looked like he hadn't shaved, bathed, or had a conscious thought, in decades. Day figured he probably smelled as bad as he looked, but couldn't tell over the other aromas generated by the clientele in general and the smells wafting from the various foodstuffs being consumed. Before she could turn her attention to measuring the mettle of the person on her left, the bartender turned its attention onto her. "Whaddya wanna drink?" The voice was cold and if Day hadn't recognized the bartender as another Spotted Menotroid she would have been offended by the brusque manner.

She ordered a Glenfiddich, neat. "Got nunna that," the Menotroid sneered. "Dunno what it is." Day told him it was Scotch whiskey from Earth and was offered Super Crown Royal instead. Rather than point out the difference, she ordered a tall Spiritsapper. The bartender gave her a dirty look and went to fix the drink. Menotroids may have been lacking in many social virtues, Day noticed, but they made excellent bartenders. The six tentacles allowed it to serve multiple customers at once, which was a great time saver.

Something jogged her left arm and almost pushed her off the stool. Day turned to look at the person who had done it; it was a pseudo human, one of those semi-men grown specifically to perform menial tasks on fledgling colonies. She wondered what such a creature was doing in Chuckie's, but didn't get the chance to dwell on the thought. The thing, obviously under the influence of something, pushed her again.

"Excuse me," she said to it, "But you're bothering me." The pseudo human leered at her, its eyes traveling up and down her from her feet to the top of her head. They paused as they passed her breasts and Day had no doubt what thoughts were running through what passed for a brain in the poor creature. It made her feel dirty.

"I'm trying to bodder you," the pseudo human replied, drool starting to form at the edge of its mouth. "I like you. Youze nice looking!"

"Thanks, but I'm not interested." Her Spiritsapper was placed on the bar in front of her and the bartender demanded four stollars. She reached into her purse, making sure no one could see the interesting things she had in it, and she pulled out a five stollar note. Before she could hand it to the bartender, though, the pseudo human pushed a bill in front of her.

"My treat for you," it said, "Just like yoor going to be my treat for today." Day groaned inside. She palmed a microstunner and removed her hand from inside her purse. She dropped it to her side and turned to face the creature.

"Look," she said, "I appreciate the drink and the compliment, but I'm really not interested. Understand?" She turned back to the bar and reached for her drink. The pseudo human reached out and grabbed her hand.

"Don be like that, missy," he slobbered. "I show you real good time. Wanna see my equipment?" It reached downward with its other hand, the leer becoming more pronounced and the drool trickling down its chin, and caressed her behind clumsily and roughly.

"Get your hand off me right now," she ordered, standing up. She stole a quick glance around. A few people had turned to face them, but nobody appeared interested in getting involved. She motioned with her head toward the bartender, who was watching them with a bored expression on his face. "Hey," she said to him, "Don't you guys have a bouncer here? This guy's annoying me!"

The Spotted Menotroid shook his head, his tentacles remaining busy with their various tasks. "Nope," he said, "As long as you all pays your bills, and damages, Chuckie's happy." He gave a quick, unimpressed glance at the pseudo human, turned, and walked to the other end of the bar, carrying drinks.

The pseudo human snorted. "See, missy, these people don't care 'bout you." Its grip on her behind tightened. "But I do!" It pulled her closer and lifted her face toward its, a drop of slobber dripping from its chin and landing on her arm.

Day had had enough. She raised the microstunner and gave it a squeeze. The beam caught the pseudo human amidships. Startled, but not stunned, or at least any more stunned than it had been to start with, it let go of her and clutched at its chest. A blue spot appeared where the beam hit, growing wider and deeper in color as the microstunner blast continued. A funny look, as if the creature's dim brain had become overloaded, came over its face, and it slumped backward, knocking the next patron from its bar stool. They landed in a pile on the floor, where the creature twitched sickeningly, then was still. Around her, people who'd watched the incident with mild interest lost that interest again and went back to tending their own affairs.

"Took quite a shot, didn't it?" said a voice behind Day. She spun around to face a tall, male human who stood there smiling at her. "Disgusting things, really," he continued, "Though it's not their fault."

Day looked at the newcomer suspiciously. "Who the hell are you?"

she demanded. He was dressed casually, though not poorly, and she noticed a pair of powerspecs poking from his chest pocket. He had a kind face, though she knew that didn't mean she could relax.

He sized her up the same way before replying. "You seem to know how to handle yourself. I'm impressed." He stuck out a hand. "Gerard Dupuis, at your service."

Day glared at him. "At my service," she mocked. "Where the hell were you a minute ago, when I could have used some service?"

"I was over there," he said, pointing to a booth. "I really was coming over to help, but I see you didn't need me after all." He looked at the microstunner she still held. "You've obviously been in places like this before."

She relaxed a little. "Yeah," she said, "Once. Anyway, thanks for showing up. You're the only gentleman here."

Dupuis shook his head. "Oh, no. Actually, the person I'm with is the gentleman. It was her idea that I help you." Day looked toward the booth Dupuis had indicated, and could just make out a small, birdlike creature with humanoid arms, sitting partially hidden in the shadows. She thought it must be an Avitite.

"Well, thank you both."

"You are most welcome," Dupuis agreed. "Why don't you join us? You can thank Trillia yourself."

Day accepted the invitation, as much to disappear into the woodwork as anything, and rescued her Spiritsapper from the bar.

"A little help here, please."

Day then noticed the man on the floor under the pseudo human, trapped by the bulk of the creature. She rolled the body off him with her foot, releasing the man. Then she and Dupuis threaded their way through the mess of tables and over to the booth, where the little Avitite moved to the center of the curved bench to make room. Dupuis and Day sat down, Day across the table from the others.

"I'm afraid you have me at a loss," Dupuis remarked. "I've told you who I am, but I don't know anything about you other than what I've observed. You're obviously a very capable lady who can fend for herself. But do you have a name?"

Day frowned. "Well, in my line of work you travel a lot and it pays to know some self defense." Then she smiled at them, her eyes taking in both Dupuis and the bird creature. "I'm Bonnie Day, and thanks again for trying to help." The Avitite chirped a series of squeaky notes; it was the first time she'd heard one of them speak, or whatever it was they did. It was a very pretty sound, though of course the literal meaning of the notes was totally lost on her. She could guess the creature's mood, however, from its morose expression – unless that was they way they all looked.

Dupuis translated. "Trillia says it seemed the right thing to do. She understands Language, but her physiology makes in impossible for her to form the words." Day wasn't surprised; she doubted she could speak Avitite, either, which made them even. Good thing she came with a built-in translator.

"Forgive me, I've never met an Avitite before," Day said to the creature. "It's a pleasure to meet you. Forgive me my inquisitiveness, but am I correct in noticing that you seem depressed?" Trillia trilled a few sweet-sounding tones, but her eyes belied the beauty of the utterance.

"You are very perceptive, Miss Day. Trillia is, indeed, feeling down on account of getting bounced from Littman's today," Dupuis said. "We came here to drown her sorrows."

Day's ears perked up at the name, and she watched with interest as the Avitite emitted another series of chirps, twittering on a few seconds more before sticking her long and slender beak into the tall glass in front of her.

"Trillia says she's glad to know you and apologizes in advance for being depressing." Dupuis stuck out his hand once again and this time she shook it. "And I'm glad to know you, too, Bonnie Day. A toast." He raised his glass. The birdthing, who had raised her head to look at Bonnie, stuck her beak back into the glass and made sucking noises.

Day hoisted her glass. "Cheers." She took a sip of what turned out to be the worst Spiritsapper in history, grimaced, and put the glass back on the table and pushed it away from her. "Yikes! What do they use here, synthetic pernooie?"

"Old Glammer," said Dupuis, motioning in the general direction of the bartender, "Probably never heard of whatever that thing is you're drinking. Neither have I."

She told him what it was called and offered him a taste, which he refused. The Avitite shook its head, too, when Day moved her glass toward her as well.

"Spiritsapper." She rhymed off the ingredients, ending with "And real pernooie. Not this slop. Mix them together, meld the molecules, and serve over water ice. It originated at the Park Hotel in Murracum."

Dupuis' eyebrows arched and the bird creature gave a start. "On Wendalow?" Day nodded. The Avitite shook her head and took another drink. "You have been around." He took another sip from his own poison. "So, what is your line of work that brings you here? Liquor inspector?" His eyes glittered.

Day laughed. "I wish. They wouldn't have to pay me for that! Let's just say I'm a troubleshooter." She changed the subject away from herself. "Trillia, why did you lose your job?" Perhaps she could be pumped for information. Trillia chirped back at her.

"She doesn't want to talk about it. You know how it is." The birdthing took another drink. Dupuis continued. "She gave five years to those bandits, five good years as their chief auditor."

"Hmm," Day added helpfully.

"Yeah, well I've know her longer than that. She's a straight shooter. Anyway, she told me a while back that she came across some, well, discrepancies in the books, things that couldn't be reconciled. Materials came in but supposedly never went out, and never showed up in inventory. You know."

"Yeah. Shrinkage."

"Okay," Dupuis agreed. The Avitite evidently decided to tell the rest of the story herself, because she chimed in with a series of chirps and twitters that caused Dupuis to switch from storyteller to interpreter. "Well, Trillia says a certain amount is normal, though still illegal, but there was lots more of that kind of stuff than there should have been. She went to Littman himself with the information and was told 'Thank you very much, now shut up and mind your own business.'"

"Sounds like a nice fellow, this Littman."

"Never met him," said Dupuis. "Don't want to. Anyway, Trillia, she figures it's a theft ring and digs into it a bit more. She finds out that there are whole jobs going out uninvoiced." He paused while the Avitite took another suck with her built-in straw, then took up the story again when the chirps re-commenced. "She says there are millions of stollars going out the doors without showing up on the books. So she went to Littman again, thinking he'd want to know about all this." Trillia gave another cascade of chirps, then fell silent. "And he fires her!" Dupuis took a long draw on his drink.

Day, trying to hide her interest, pressed the service button on the table and looked around for a waiter. A dour looking human started coming toward them. She looked back at Trillia. "It sounds like you were doing the guy a favor and he threw it right back in your face. That's tough." The waiter arrived and she ordered a beer. The others ordered repeats of their own drinks.

Day's mind was racing. If this creature knew the ifs, ands, or buts, maybe she knew about the ship Day was tracking. She leaned forward conspiratorially. "You really got a raw deal and I don't blame you for being mad." She received chirps in reply, and from their tone Day required no translation.

Then the drinks came and Day reached into her purse and brought out enough money to pay the tab. She gave it to the waiter and he went away. She took a sip of her beer and leaned in close to the others again. She looked the birdthing squarely in the eyes. "I might have a way you can get back at Littman and help me at the same time. Interested?"

# STOREBOUGHT INFORMATION
## -- Chapter 13

Bonnie Day pulled out a fake I.D. and held it up. "I never did tell you what I do for a living," she said. Dupuis and Trillia looked at the card and saw her picture swim into existence on its surface, along with various misleading bits of information about her position as an investigator for the Co-operative Body of Revenue Generation. It was a totally convincing piece of fiction that would have persuaded even another tax department official. After a few seconds the image disappeared and they stopped looking at it. They turned their gaze back to Day and stared at her with highly piqued interest. She had them on the hook. Now, to reel them in.

Trillia trilled at her, and Dupuis translated "What do you have in mind?"

Day started reeling. "Look, I'm here because the Co-op has reason to believe Littman hasn't been paying his taxes, corporate or personal. I'm here to dig around and see if there's enough evidence to warrant a full scale audit." She put the ID badge back into her purse and took a long, leisurely draw on her draft while gazing serenely at the Avitite and the human.

She didn't have long to wait. In a moment the Avitite began chirruping rapidly and excitedly at her and Dupuis had to ask her to slow down so he'd have time to translate. "Trillia says there's a lot she can tell you. That sort of thing went on all the time," he said, undoubtedly paraphrasing. "She says she can give you enough data to put Littman out of business."

"Sounds good to me," Day agreed, "But all I really need is a couple of highlights I can use to justify bringing in reinforcements. Maybe some of the bigger jobs that went out under the table?"

Trillia chirped again, her beak nodding up and down with excitement.

"She says she's got anything you need," Dupuis translated. "Now I have a question for you."

"Yes?"

"Since Trillia's doing you such a big favor and since she's out of work, what's in this for her?"

"What does she want?" The creature let out another series of noises then, with what seemed to Day a self satisfied smirk, shut up abruptly and sat there staring at her, blinking her large eyes expectantly. "Well?" Day said.

"She wants ten thousand stollars. She didn't say so, but I think it should be in cash."

Day smiled. "Don't you think I'm the wrong person to be talking about untraceable cash to?" Dupuis' expression for a few seconds was as if his life were flashing before his eyes as he realized his gaffe. Good! It would reinforce her story.

"Uh, well, okay, maybe a check would do," Dupuis stammered lamely.

"That's okay. I'll get you the cash from a money machine," she laughed. "I'm sure Trillia won't mind signing a receipt for me?" Trillia chose that moment to put her beak back into her glass for another sip of drink. "After all, it is income and has to be declared." She hoped she wasn't laying it on too thick, but the pair seemed to be buying everything she said. She looked around the smoky room and noticed that the pseudo human she'd knocked out earlier was struggling back to his feet, swaying uneasily. Though his eyes appeared to be quite glazed, he was looking around the bar and Day figured she knew for whom he was searching. She stood up. "Well, we certainly can't conclude our business here. I have to find a money machine and I'm sure you don't carry this proof you speak of with you. Right?" The bird creature nodded its long beak up and down.

"You're right," Dupuis added. He stood up and the Avitite hopped onto his shoulder. Day smiled inwardly at the sight; it reminded her of an old pirate from some old viddy, with its parrot perched on his shoulder, though of course the Avitite was larger. Dupuis wriggled out from behind the table and headed for the exit, Day following closely behind. As she disappeared into the hallway that led outside, she stole a quick glance back to see the pseudo human still rubbernecking the room, apparently unaware of her.

Outside, they stood blinking for a moment as their eyes became accustomed to the sunshine. Trillia suggested through Dupuis that they go back to her place and she'd give Day a copy of the Littman file. Dupuis suggested they stop by a money machine first. Day agreed and they went around to the rear of Chuckie's and got into Dupuis' vehicle, a beat up, nondescript ground car the sight of which made Day cringe. It looked quite unsafe, but she kept her mouth shut and got in the rear seat compartment anyway, making sure to fasten the ratty-looking seatbelt firmly around her waist. Dupuis and Trillia got into the front, Dupuis behind the old fashioned steering yoke, and they left the parking lot.

The trip into Trillia's neighborhood only took a few minutes and Day spent the time sightseeing out the window. She ended up glad for the short duration of the ride, not only because of the decrepit conveyance, but because the sightseeing was lousy. It seemed as if that part of Panadar City could have been in any city on any industrialized planet – ugly, dirty and noisy, and she very quickly lost interest in the view. Then they pulled around a corner and Dupuis brought the car to a halt with a lurch outside a blue money machine kiosk. "Will this one do?" he asked, turning around in the seat to look at Day.

"It should do just fine," she told him. "I'll be right back." And she was. "Okay, let's go," she said when she got back into the car ten thousand stollars richer. She strapped on the seatbelt as the car left the curb and in a few minutes they pulled up outside an apartment building. "You live here?" she said.

The building in question was a trifle more luxurious than she had anticipated. Since the Avitite was obviously not well to do, she had assumed it would have had a more modest nest, but the classy singles condominium development in front of her must have come with a high rent.

Dupuis must have noticed her surprise. "Nice place, huh? I helped Trillia find it." He frowned. "Avitites have a lot of trouble finding places to stay 'cause of what they do to them. I guess the owners have trouble cleaning up after they move out."

"Really?" remarked Day.

Dupuis continued "Anyway, I helped her arrange for an extra big damage deposit and she covers the extra rent by doing the books for the company that owns the place. It works out well for 'em both."

"Sounds like an ideal arrangement," Day agreed. She followed Dupuis and Trillia into the building and they went up the elevator tube to the ninety-fifth floor in a matter of seconds. Day hated those tubes, especially the flip flop in the stomach when the field first took control. On the way up she got the idea to ask the Xannyk people if they could figure out a way to get around that stomach wrench like they'd done for the Jump trauma.

Or maybe she'd talk to Jing and they could share the patent....

Then they were on Trillia's floor and she put the thought away. Trillia's door was unique in that its thumbpad identifier had been replaced by a little voice recognizer mounted about half a meter from the floor. The birdthing hooted and hollered, the door slid open and they went inside.

"I can see why some landlords could get upset about Avitites," Day said as she got her first view of the condo. The place looked like a huge, indoor nest, with sticks and twigs spread over the floor and branches rising up floor to ceiling. Several holes had been cut into the walls between the rooms to make room for branches long and stout enough to support the Avitite's weight. A couch and an armchair graced the living room, but they were old and much damaged from having been gripped by talons. Day could only imagine what had been done to tailor the kitchen and bathroom to the creature...

Dupuis went over to the armchair and sat down. Day sat on the couch. Trillia chirped something and went into another room. "She says make yourself at home and she'll be right back with the data," Dupuis said.

"Nice place," Day said, "Though I can see why she'd have trouble renting."

"I can't understand it myself," Dupuis said. "I mean, sure she makes a mess, but she's willing to pay for it. Most places don't give a damn, though."

"A lot of landlords probably just don't want the hassle," Day suggested, "Or to be forced into using conscious thought."

Trillia came back carrying a data card in her beak. She dropped it in Day's lap and waited. Day thanked her and pulled the cash from her purse, handed – or beaked – it to the creature. The Avitite took it and leapt up onto a branch and stuck it in a leafy space between two short branches. She chirruped happily and began preening.

"She says thanks."

"I gathered that. My pleasure," Day replied, looking at the card. "I don't suppose I can check out this information before leaving all that cash here?"

"You know where to find her if you aren't satisfied," Dupuis said. "She says that card only has the information for the three biggest jobs she found. She says it's all you'll need."

"Fine. But what are they?"

More chirruping, then Dupuis said "Two jobs were for the refitting of a couple of luxury yachts for some bigwig on Gault. You know, that place with all the casinos?"

"I've heard of it," Day said. "And the other one?"

Trillia chirped and chirped, then went back to combing her beak through her feathers. "The other was a whole fleet conversion, freighters, a bunch of shuttles. Other stuff." More chirruping. "She says they did something like a complete refit and then Littman turned around and sold all the old parts as brand new in other jobs. None of it went on the books. Anyway," he pointed, "It's all on that card. Hope it helps."

Day's heart belied her serene exterior. "I'm sure it will. Thanks. The Co-operative will be very grateful." She reached into her purse and pulled out a blank piece of paper and a stylus, and began scribbling. "This isn't an official form, you realize," she said as she wrote, "But it's legal." She stopped writing and held up the sheet. "Now, if I can just get you to autograph this receipt our business is complete."

Trillia flew from the branch and landed in front of Day. She took the receipt from Day's hand with her beak and put in on the floor, then read it over. She chirped and made some scratching marks on the paper with Day's stylus.

"Thanks," Day said, folding the receipt and putting it away. "I'll see that you get a copy." She stood up. "Well, I guess I don't need to bother either of you any longer. Thanks again for all your help." Trillia chirped happily.

"Just make sure you nail that Littman fellow," Dupuis said. "He's got it coming."

"He certainly seems to," Day agreed. "I'll do my best." She started for the door. Dupuis rose and began to follow. "I can find my own way out," she said. "Thanks again."

Dupuis said goodbye and the Avitite chirruped what Day assumed was the same. She took the lift tube back down to ground level and went out onto the street to find a cab. It took a few minutes, but she flagged one down presently and ordered the auto driver to take her back to the spaceport.

"Welcome home, Bonnie," greeted the computer. "I hope you had a profitable trip."

"I think so," Day said. "I hope so, anyway." She took the card from her purse and inserted it into the slot on the control panel. "What do you make of this?"

There was the shortest of pauses, then the computer replied "It's a file named 'Littman Conversions -- Unreconciled Work' and coded to 'P. Trillia Aviallatia'. An interesting name."

"She's an Avitite," Day said.

"Really? Then the name is appropriate," the computer replied. "I have never met an Avitite."

"Me neither, till now. They're very pretty. But I couldn't understand a thing she said."

"That's not surprising, Bonnie. My records show that Avitite speech is incompatible with human speech, even Language." Day grunted.

"Yeah, well, I don't care about that. What's in the file?"

"The file is brand new, in case you're interested. It was made fifty three minutes ago, edited down from a larger file, according to its structure."

"So?"

"I thought you'd want to know."

Day lightened up. "Sorry."

"No offence. The file lists two companies and gives an entire accounting including design, inventory, progress reports, etcetera. Would you like a printout?"

"Please." A long tongue of paper started coming out silently from the printslot. It fell into the receiving bin, tearing itself in pages of somewhat normal size to facilitate Day's reading. She grabbed the first few pages and glanced at them quickly. It did look as if it was all there. Day thought Littman shouldn't have crossed the little Avitite because she had a lot more on him than she had suspected. Littman was probably one of those people who thought their little empires were the hub of the galaxy and treated everyone around them as if they were somewhat inferior. She'd met the type a thousand times. Well, he'd misjudged Trillia.

Day smiled. It was too bad she wasn't really with the Co-operative Body of Revenue Generation. She had enough to really nail Littman's hide to the wall. She should probably send a copy to the Co-op....

On the other hand. "This is pretty good stuff," she remarked. "A person could make good money peddling information like this."

"It could be quite valuable to many people," the computer agreed.

Then, Bingo! "Look at this! Littman reconfigured four Class IV freighters. Turned the things into battleships. Look at these work orders! Blasters, power packs, hammocks, rations, the guy's built a war fleet!"

"I don't mean to interrupt, Bonnie," said the computer, "But those plans of the shuttles match my records of the one we've brought with us. The video you shot inside the ship matches the interior plans, too. And notice on pages eight and forty-three the absence of plans for the drive systems."

Day found the pages, stared hard at them. "It says 'Drive components and related systems to be user installed,'" she read. "'Affected sections of the ship are restricted to authorized user personnel.'"

"I'm surprised at that," said the computer. "Why would they not want to have all the work done by Littman, especially since they're there already?"

"Maybe whoever it is didn't want to give out his technology or tip his hand for free," Day said.

"I hadn't thought of that. Of course, money means nothing to me."

"As a computer, you're probably better off that way," Day said. "But it means something to a lot of people, including me." She riffled through the collection of papers that had filled the bin, hoping some most important bit of information would leap off the page. "We've got ourselves a major bingo here," Day breathed. She shuffled through some more sheets. "But who was it for?" she said.

"There is a name, but it doesn't match anything in the records."

"What is it? Where?"

"There is a name on the electronic letterhead that begins the plans. The plans, evidently, were not drawn up at Littman, but were delivered there. The work orders, progress reports, and the other sections, are Littman's."

"How can you tell?"

"The datings and source codes are different."

"Oh." Handy gadget to have around. Day had found the sheet of paper the computer meant. She looked at the name. "What is this?"

"Unfortunately, it's gibberish," said the computer. "I can make no logical sense of it."

"Could it be code?"

"Possibly. Let me analyze it." There was a few seconds pause, though it seemed interminable to Day, as the computer ran the nonsense letters through its processors, trying to match them with a known code. "I believe I have found what you colloquially refer to as a major bingo, Bonnie," it said at last and a new sheet of paper was printed out.

Day tore it from the bin before all four of its corners had touched down. She stared at the name. It was unfamiliar, but it made perfect sense. "Who the hell is Trader Vanday Makteer?" she asked.

"He is a Viknu, now of the planet Taddayoosh," the computer replied. "In fact, he owns the planet Taddayoosh and has holdings in various parts of the Co-operative. He is worth a tidy sum. If I were to use another of your colloquialisms I would say he is a major player."

"No kidding! I could think of a few planets I wouldn't minding having as part of my holdings. A little place in the Fourth Sector comes to mind," she said almost under her breath.

"I didn't know you were interested in real estate, Bonnie. That doesn't appear in your file."

"There's a lot that's not in my file" Day said shortly. "Anyway, it's not so much an interest in real estate as an urge to settle down somewhere. I get tired of living out of a suitcase."

"Out of a suitcase?"

Day laughed. "On the road, so to speak. No real home." She looked around, at the plush Xannyk interior. "Though I have to admit you make a fine suitcase!"

"Thank you, I think," said the computer.

"So this creature Makteer is a bit of a high roller," Day said, getting back to the subject.

"It would seem. His portfolio is quite extensive. He is almost responsible for keeping the economy of his sector going single-handedly."

As the printed sheets of the Makteer file fell into the bin Day picked them up and looked them over. Eventually she whistled. "Well, I'd say this guy looks like he's worth checking out. Taddayoosh, you say?"

"I have computed a course, but it's an involved one. We'll need four Jumps and the total one way trip requires forty standard days."

"Then we'd better get going," Day said. "Let's pay this Makteer fellow a visit." She sat on the couch and put her feet on the coffee table. "And don't forget to pick up that shuttle. I think I've figured out how I can use it."

Day watched the shifting patterns of light idly as they ran across the main screen while the yacht tended to the business of readying for space and getting cleared through traffic control. She closed her eyes and lost herself in thought.

Makteer sounded like he was exactly the sort of person with the wherewithal to pull off the job and make it work. He was filthy rich, probably among the top twenty in the Co-operative, and apparently with an ego the size of space. He would make a formidable adversary; she'd better be sharp. She'd poke about Taddayoosh, gather enough dirt to call in the Marines, then get back out and retire again.

"Traffic control signaling. We have clearance to leave the planet," said the computer.

"Good. Let's do it," Day replied.

"Clearing the pad." Day asked for an outside view and watched the surface of the planet drop away below her as the yacht launched skyward. In a few moments the sky got dark and the stars came out as the ship reached space. "Panadar says we are cleared to leave their control," the Xannyk informed Day, then "We are now leaving orbit."

"Good," Day acknowledged. "Get that shuttle, then let's get on our way." She got up and went into the galley to fix herself a drink. Perhaps she should compose a note to Auntie, bring her up to date. Makteer's file was pretty convincing, as far as she was concerned, but knowing Auntie she'd pooh-pooh it and tell her to come back with some hard evidence, something that would stand up in court. "Fine," Day muttered as the cook'n'munch produced a steaming cup of coffee. "You want it, you'll get it."

# TADDAYOOSH -- Chapter 14

"We have arrived, Bonnie," the computer said forty days later. They were on the edge of Taddayoosh's system, far enough from the planet itself to be reasonably sure they weren't detected by any watchers. The main screen showed their position relative to Taddayoosh, on a Astrographix system chart the Xannyk had in memory.

"Good," Day grunted absently. She was preoccupied with getting the final tabs on her spacesuit connected properly so she could leave the ship. Murphy's Law, unfortunately, had stepped in and was preventing her gloved fingers from completing the relatively simple job she'd done without difficulty so many times in the past. Finally, almost reaching the point of exasperation as her fingers fumbled with the fasteners, she cursed and said to the computer "I sure wish you had arms so you could help me with this stupid catch!"

"You should get a robot servant," the computer remarked.

"Do you know how much they want for one of those things?"

"The standard equipped Smithy McLeod CyberManservant lists for seventy thousand stollars in the current catalogue," the computer informed her as she finally managed to get the last catch caught. She shook her head in relief and reached for her fishbowl hat.

"You know what else I could buy if I had seventy grand to throw around?"

"Would you like a list printed out, Bonnie?"

"It was a rhetorical question."

"I see. Then I will put that file back into memory."

"Do that," Day said as she pulled the helmet over her head. She slid it around the quarter turn required to seal it to the space suit and switched on the radio. "Testing."

"I receive you fine, Bonnie," said the computer.

"Good. Let's go. You remember my instructions?"

"I don't forget things, Bonnie. I am to remain here until I hear from you, up to a time limit of two weeks. I have to object again to that last stipulation."

"Just do it. I want to know where to find you."

"But why must I wait that long to contact headquarters if you go missing?"

"Because I don't know how long this will take and I don't want my elbow jiggled," Day said. "Besides, if I need you badly enough I'll contact you. I'm not totally incompetent."

"I didn't mean to insinuate that you were, Bonnie. But are you familiar with something called Murphy's Law?"

Day laughed. "You better believe I am. But what's a computer doing quoting it?" There was only silence from the Xannyk, so Day said "Thanks for the concern, but I'll be alright. I've done this type of thing before." She opened the inner airlock door, entered the lock. "I'm glad to see the patch job holding up," she remarked.

"It will hold through a minimum of two hundred seventy-three cycles," said the computer. "Goodbye, Bonnie. And good luck."

"Thanks." The inner door closed behind her and the lights on the panel near it activated as the atmosphere was drained from the little airlock. When the lights were all red there came a low, muffled rumble inside the ship as the outer door opened. One of the lights turned green to indicate the door had finished moving.

Day stepped out of the airlock and, once her feet left the inside of the yacht and she was no longer bound by its gravity field, eased open her thrusters gently, allowing them just enough juice to push her away from the yacht slowly. A few meters away hung the little shuttle, looking no worse for wear from its long drag and push across the Co-operative. Day propelled herself toward the shuttle and, shortly, braked to a stop outside its airlock. "Is it powered up and ready?"

"All my remote readouts show her to be functional in every way," she heard through the speaker in her helmet. Good. She went inside. She waited before taking off her helmet until the airlock's cycle had completed and the inner door had opened to let her into the cramped interior of the small ship. She hung the helmet on the rack near the lock and went over to the control panel. She turned on the radio and established contact with the Xannyk. "Okay," she said, "You ready to monitor me?"

"Certainly, Bonnie. Are you ready to proceed?"

"Not quite. I want to get out of this suit first." She looked over the panel to make sure she knew how to drive the ship, then, satisfied there were no arcane secrets to its operation, wriggled out of the suit. She hung it by the helmet and went back and sat in the pilot's chair. "Computer," she barked.

"Yes, Bonnie?"

"Not you, this computer."

"Sorry."

"Operating," came the rather dull sounding reply. "What is your wish?"

"Are you ready to go?" Day asked, noting in passing that the computer sounded typically configured, which meant it was boring. If you wanted personality in your cybernetics it cost more than people were generally willing to pay. Day looked around the interior of the cramped ship. She'd miss the frills.

To Day, it took an interminably long time before the computer replied "Everything is in the green. Where do you wish to go?"

Day said "Do you know where Taddayoosh is?" There was another long pause as the ship scanned its memory and matched what it found in the star charts with what it saw around it. "I am presently located here," the monitor lit up with a representation of space, with a single bright point of light highlighted. "Taddayoosh is here." Another point lit. "An approximate two day journey. What is your wish?"

"I wish," Day said, "To go into orbit around it."

"Program activated. Arrival at Taddayoosh in forty seven hours, thirteen minutes. What is your wish?"

"I wish," Day said, "That you'd come up with another prompt than 'what is your wish'."

"I can use whatever prompt you program. What is your wish?"

Day thought for a moment, trying to decide what sort of prompt wouldn't wear thin very quickly. Then it struck her. "Your new prompt will be one second of silence. Do you understand?"

"I will prompt with one second of silence."

Day smiled. "That's better. Now contact the yacht behind us and start relaying your telemetry to it. Keep in contact until we're six hours away from Taddayoosh."

"Contact established. Inter-ship voice contact is open as well."

"I know. How you doing back there, Xannyk?" Day said.

"Conditions here are unchanged from a moment ago, Bonnie," the yacht said immediately. "The data I'm receiving from your location indicate you'll arrive at Taddayoosh precisely when that computer said."

Day nodded. "Good. Talk to you later. Keep your eyes peeled."

"I assume that to be a colloquialism for me to remain alert. You may assume that as a given."

"I thought I could. Consider voice contact now broken unless I holler 'Xannyk!'" That would prevent both computers from jumping to attention every time she called the shuttle's. "Computer," she said.

"Computer?" Day said again, then remembered that the new prompt was in effect. "Computer, answer me," she said.

"Dammit," Day said, then shrugged it off. Silence was still better than that servile 'What is your wish?' prompt she'd replaced. The computer would be listening even though it hadn't spoken a reply, so she continued. "Do you know how to make a real Spiritsapper?"

Taddayoosh swam in the monitor, a large, lush ball hanging in space ahead of them. Day opted for a straight in approach rather than mess with going into orbital traffic; it would give ground control less time to react to them and, though anyone competent should still have no trouble following their progress, Day didn't want to give them any more opportunity than necessary. She scanned the computer's map of the planet, located what was labeled as Makteer's palace, and instructed the shuttle to land at the port nearest it.

Taddayoosh looked like an interesting planet, a great place for a holiday in the sun, but that would have to wait. Day ordered the computer to switch the view from the map to an exterior view and watched as the ship nosed into the atmosphere and headed down toward the extensive cloud cover that sat over Makteer's domain.

"Shuttle fourteen this is ground control," came a voice from the speaker. "You haven't filed an approach plan. What's going on." So they recognized the ship. Good. That beat being blasted out of existence as an invader. She opened a frequency.

"Sorry, I didn't know the local rules. I'm coming in for landing at...just a moment." She called up the port's co-ordinates from the computer and read them into the microphone.

"We know that. We can see your trajectory. Who are you and what are you doing in one of our shuttles?"

"Name's Becky Farm," she replied, "And I'm bringing this shuttle here so you can buy it back from me. I won it off one of your folk in New Vegas. Seems he thought a full house was a pretty good hand." Day smiled. "'Course I had four of a kind and I don't take checks."

There was silence at the other end for a moment, then Day was treated to a terse "Stand by." She remained seated as she waited impatiently for the ground controllers to decide which direction was up.

The silence dragged on interminably until, bored with the wait, she decided to stir things up some more. "Anyone still alive down there?" she asked, her voice exuding innocent good intentions. "I'm still alive up here, you know."

"I said stand by," came the terse reply. "We're looking into it."

"Looking into what?" she said. "I'm here with your ship and I want to return it to you. For a reasonable price, of course. What's so odd about that?" There was no reply. Day could imagine the people scrambling around dirtside, trying to figure out what to do. She could only assume, and hope, they were passing the news of her arrival on to higher authority. With, luck word would get right up to Makteer, though he probably had so many layers of underlings below him he was well insulated from such mundane goings on as the arrival of a lost shuttle.

Then again, maybe she could stir things up even more. "Look I was told by your hired hand that this ship belonged to someone named Trader Vanday Makteer before it was mine. Well I want to talk to him about selling it back." She paused, then said "I need money a heckuva lot more than I need a dinky little ship like this. So whaddya say? And don't pawn me off on some underling, either." She was actually enjoying herself; tossing out bait had always been an agreeable pastime, though she liked the reeling in process even more.

"Sensors indicate two vessels approaching at high speed," reported the shuttle. Day ordered them shown on the screen and, when they appeared, saw that they were military-style interceptors bristling with firepower. It looked like she'd have an escort to the surface.

"Hello you goons outside," she said pleasantly, "Are you here to see me safely to ground?"

"You are ordered to fall into formation between us, outworlder," came a gruff, masculine voice. Day told the shuttle to comply with the order.

They continued groundward, but in a longer arc that, according to the data, would take them far from the spaceport.

"Where are you taking me?" Day asked. "This isn't the way to the spaceport."

"Just stay in formation," she was ordered. "And don't ask questions if you don't want to get hurt."

"That's no way to treat a lady," she replied with the right touch of disgust in her voice. "I'm coming, I'm coming. As if I have any choice! Boy, you try to help out this Makteer fellow and all you get is abuse. This is the last time I do any favors."

"Be quiet and follow." Day shut up, grinning from ear to ear. She wondered how many armed guards there'd be waiting for her and how long they'd keep her cooling her heels before someone in authority deigned to see her.

Suddenly, they broke through the cloud cover and Day got a

beautiful look at the surface of Taddayoosh. She was flying down a lush, green valley through which a middling wide stream meandered on its way to who knew where without checking a map. Day thought it would have made a wonderful location for a spa, the natural beauty still unspoiled by civilization, at least in the immediate area. She had the computer scan up and down the valley in both directions, then froze the monitor on an awe-inspiring sight directly ahead of her about fifty kilometers away.

Built right into the mountainside, and looking almost as if it were actually part of the surrounding terrain, was a huge castle complete with spires and minarets, though they weren't the traditional towering structures from old Earth tales. Rather, they seemed to rise gracefully from the mountainside, trying to look as much like natural formations as possible. They reminded Day of the hoodoos she'd seen in pictures a long time ago. She whistled appreciatively. It was a heckuvan engineering job, and if she'd been wearing a hat she'd have doffed it to the people responsible for the construction.

No matter what she might find out about Makteer, she couldn't fault his taste. The palace was obviously opulent, but it blended with the environment in a way that was a marvel to behold. Day was surprised; she'd have expected something much more gaudy from someone with a profile like Makteer's.

"I am receiving incoming data," said the computer. Day came back to reality.

"What is it?"

"I am being ordered to call approach vector seventeen from my memory."

"What's that?"

"Approach vector seventeen is a landing trajectory that will bring me in to the Palace port. It is a standard approach from this direction and I have used it many times before."

"Then what are you waiting for?" Day said. "Call it up and get on with it."

They were whizzing over the treetops, still several hundred meters from ground level but scant meters above the highest branches. The plants blurred in the screen, so fast was the ship's velocity in relation to the ground. Then there was a large clearing and the ship immediately slowed dramatically and started nosing toward a lighted square in the center of the open area. Moving processions of lights pointed toward a small area on one side of the pad and the shuttle turned that way, heading in a long swoop toward a landing. When it was obvious the little ship was committed to touching down at the indicated spot, the accompanying interceptors broke off and veered away, disappearing from Day's view as they headed away.

"Stand by," said the computer.

The castle swelled in the viewer, then it left her field of vision as the shuttle nosed down toward the landing pad and it filled the viewscreen instead. Day thought the shuttle was coming in too fast and braced herself for the crash that seemed inevitable. Then, when it appeared too late for a safe landing, the nose shot upward until it was level with the ground, bringing Makteer's palace back into view. Forward motion bled away in seconds and with a whine and a groan the shuttle settled downward onto the pad and was still.

Day could hear the engines winding down as both of the airlock doors opened and the sickly sweet smell of what were undoubtedly tropical plants wafted through the opening. Day got up from the chair, went into the airlock, and poked her head outside. She blinked in the bright sunshine and shaded her eyes with her hand until they became accustomed to the illumination. Then she stepped from the lock and onto the small set of stairs that had folded out from the side of the shuttle. She started walking down to the landing pad.

"Stop right there and petrify!" came a command from her right. She stopped and turned to look. She found the inevitable reception committee. This one was made up of about ten burly humans, each armed to the teeth and pointing heavy duty blasters in her direction.

"Whaddya mean putrefy?" she called out. "I don't know what you're talking about!"

"Don't be smart, Farm," snarled the leader. "Just stand there and don't move a bloody muscle if ya wanna stay healthy." Day complied, grateful to find her cover appeared to be working so far. Her escort reached her and deployed into a three-sided square around her, with the shuttle acting as the fourth side. The tall, tough-looking leader came to where she stood and motioned for her to continue down the steps. When she reached the bottom he told her to freeze again and proceeded to give her a thorough frisking.

"Watch it, buddy," Day said as his hands probed her, "On some planets I've visited what you're doing would be the same as a marriage proposal. And I don't want to get married just yet. I hardly know you!"

"Shut up and stand still," the man ordered. He finished the frisking, taking several of Day's favorite pieces of armament as he came across them. "That's quite a collection of heat you pack," he said when he was finished. "Expecting trouble?"

"Not really," Day replied sweetly, "But if you were single girl would you go to a strange planet without being prepared?"

"Probably not," he admitted. He motioned for one of his henchmen to come forward and the man approached them, hauling out a carrying case as he came. He scooped up Day's weapons and dropped them into it, drawing it closed and sealing it by running his fingers over the sealstrip along its mouth. He slung the bag over his left shoulder and went back to his original position, drawing a bead on Day with his blaster rifle once more.

"You people don't seem to trust me," Day remarked. "How come? And what's with all the trained apes? You think one person like me is going to beat up on all of them and run away?"

"Shut up, will you?" said the leader, exasperation in his voice. He stepped away a couple of paces and brought a communicator up to his face. He spoke some words into it that Day couldn't make out.

She measured the man and his cronies, and decided that discretion would be the better part of valor for the present. She looked over at Makteer's castle and marveled at it again. It looked even more impressive from outdoors, the evening sun glinting off its windows making it seem almost as if it were something from a child's fairy story.

A humming noise brought her back to reality and she noticed a floater approaching from the direction of the huge building. It was little more than an antigrav platform with a safety rail around its perimeter, but its purpose was plain enough. It was their transportation to wherever it was they were about to take her. Day could see the driver speaking into a headset as the floater got near, though she couldn't read the person's lips. In a moment the humming had become a low howl and the floater landed. She didn't need a map; she started heading toward it almost as soon as it had settled on its jets. The driver opened a section of guardrail and folded down some flimsy steps so Day could climb aboard, which she did, followed by the rest of her reception committee, which never ceased keeping her covered with their weapons. Trusting bunch.

Day grabbed one of the safety straps mounted on the guardrail and snapped it around her waist as the others did likewise. When all was secure, the driver folded up the steps and closed the gate. The floater rose from the pad and headed away in a gentle arc that ended up taking them toward Makteer's palace.

Day spent the trip rubbernecking around her, at the palace, the countryside, her entourage. There was little else to do; she was being swept along toward the palace and, for the present, was no longer in control of the situation. Besides, it was where she wanted to go anyway. She relaxed and enjoyed the view. It was certainly better than being cooped up in the little shuttle, and being outdoors on a lovely world like Taddayoosh was even more pleasant than being in the Xannyk; there was nothing quite like a beautiful day on a beautiful planet to raise one's spirits.

The Trader's palace loomed ahead and above them as the floater approached the mountainside. Day couldn't see any visible signs of entrances, just thousands of glassy windows reflecting pinpoints of sunlight into the lengthening shadows of Taddayoosh's late afternoon. It was a spectacular sight, a bejeweled work of art glistening for all to see. It seemed as if they were heading straight for a rock outcropping on the face of the mountain, but just when it seemed too late for them to veer away safely, a large section of what had seemed to be living rock slid sideways and disappeared into the mountain, leaving a large, gaping cave into which the floater glided easily. They were inside a subtaddayooshean parking garage not dissimilar to the one in which she'd been presented with the Xannyk. It was filled with a series of floaters and assorted beings going about their varied businesses. It wasn't exactly a hive of activity, but it would do after the loneliness of space.

Day's floater glided into a vacant stall and settled to the cave floor. They unstrapped and Day was marched down the steps and out of the garage into a wide hallway carved from the mountainside. She was walked, with armed guards in front, beside, and behind, through a series of faceless corridors until they reached a shorter one that dead-ended about fifty meters from its beginning. There were strong-looking metal doors spaced along it and they stopped by one of them. The leader of her escort pressed a thumb to the keypad and the door rumbled open. He reached inside, felt around for a moment, and the lights came on, throwing a wedge of extra illumination into the hallway. Satisfied, he motioned for Day to go into the room. She did, and the door closed behind her with a muffled thud.

Day noticed there was no handle, no keypad, no escape. There were no windows, either.

# MAKTEER -- Chapter 15

As far as cells were concerned, she'd been in worse. At least the floor wasn't dirt and there were lights and a real bathroom of sorts. It was clean and there were actually linen and soap in plain view. It was also clean of sharp objects, as she discovered after making a thorough search. Makteer obviously didn't have to worry about his prisoners suiciding or trying to come up with makeshift weapons; snapping a towel at a guard wouldn't do much to help her escape.

"Quarters!" she snorted to no one in particular. "You call these quarters? These are more like eighths!" She sat on the cot, her posterior discovering the little bed was every bit as thinly padded and uncomfortable as it looked. The pillow would have made a fair doily and the blanket looked like it would help keep her toasty warm on the surface of Gault.

Fortunately, she didn't get the opportunity to try sleeping on the arrangement. She estimated that she had been there less than two hours when a hidden speaker came to life, ordering her to step away from the door and stand in the center of the room. Instead, she stood just inside the door as it opened. Then she ducked as a net was shot into the room, but she wasn't quick enough and found herself falling to the floor, bound by the synthorope fabric as it tightened around her. She heard a laugh as her head hit the floor hard.

"That'll teach ya not to do like I tell ya," said a man as he came into the room, followed by four more goons. "This coulda been so easy, so civilized. But ya just gotta fool around." He continued walking to where Day lay, and as he got close enough, his right foot lashed out, kicking her roughly in the midsection.

A muffled "Whuff!" escaped her and she tried to wriggle away from her attacker. But the net only tightened more, cutting into her flesh. She cried out and lay still. The man came closer and stood over her, the other four crowding behind him.

"Kinda pretty, huh, Jembolla?" said one of them, a burly, nondescript type who fit in well with the surroundings and the general situation.

"Shaddap, Carl," said the first man, the one Carl had called Jembolla. He leaned closer to Day and looked into her eyes. Day stared back defiantly. "You're pretty spunky," he said, "But spunk'll only get you trouble."

"Go to hell," Day replied. Jembolla's face crinkled slowly into an evil smile and he straightened up again. He looked like he was going to turn away, but instead lashed out once more with his boot and struck Day's face hard. There was a cracking noise as her head was forced backward and sideways. Blood oozed from her nose and across her cheek. It dripped onto the cell floor. Then the five of them were on her, kicking all over her body. Day struggled, but the net only pulled tighter and she was forced to lie still and take whatever was coming.

When she came to she was on the cot. That simple fact was the first thing she noticed through the dull roar of her body, and it was several seconds in coming after consciousness had returned. If she moved, she knew, she'd regret it, so she lay still and tried to take inventory. She could feel where the net had bitten into her – could she ever! – but she could no longer feel the net. She opened her eyes, which in itself hurt, steeled herself and tried, very gingerly, to sit up. She was surprised to find she could manage it. Though every part of her complained, she swung her legs off the cot and put her feet on the floor. That was enough for now.

She rested, taking the time to look herself over as well as she could. She didn't like what she saw. She was naked. There were cuts, many quite deep, all over her arms and legs and torso and, she could only assume, everywhere else as well. The streaks of red from the open flesh served to break up the otherwise black and blue tone of her skin. It had been one hell of a working over. Admittedly, it was nothing a couple of hours in a good clinic couldn't fix up like new, but she doubted she'd receive that sort of treatment here.

She was right. By the time she'd gathered the strength to get to her feet and had made it halfway to the bathroom the hidden loudspeaker once again ordered her into the center of the room. As it turned out, she was already there, so she just stopped where she was and raised her hands above her head. Each second they were there they throbbed and she felt the pain throughout her entire being.

The cell door opened and the same group of thugs came in again, this time with blasters. The slimeballs leered as they came toward her, pausing a meter or so away from her. The leader tut-tutted as he looked her over.

"Boy, you're sure a sight to see, Missy," he said, clucking with his tongue.

"Up yours," Day replied. She lowered her arms. The movement brought no response from the men.

"Well, well, still the spunky one, eh?" the one called Carl said.

Day glared at him. "Up yours, too," she said. They marched her, naked, out of the cell and through a maze of corridors cut out of the living rock. Several times during the trip they met and passed various people going about their business. Most of them, Day noticed, seemed to go out of their way to avoid looking at her. She couldn't tell if it was because of her nudity or what, but it didn't make her any more comfortable.

Presently they arrived at a door no different from the rest, except for a large "M" on it. She was ushered inside and left alone. This door had no inside handle, either. At least the room was different from her previous cell. In fact, it was at the opposite end of the spectrum, an overstated homage to opulence designed to impress and intimidate. Day was impressed and, though she hated to admit it, she was more than a tad intimidated as well.

It wasn't a cell, more like some kind of throne room where a lord would sit in judgment over his subjects – except that there was no lord in evidence. Everything, all the rich trappings and the high technology toys present, focused on a massive divan that sprawled at the opposite end of the room from where Day stood. She could see a slight shimmering effect over and around the divan, something somehow familiar though she couldn't put her finger on it. She went over and gave it a closer look.

When she was a meter and a half from the thing she couldn't move any farther. Something had stopped her, gently. It had to be a force field of some kind. She tried pushing through it a couple of more times, but it was pointless. She could penetrate a centimeter or two at the most and the part of her that touched the field would tingle with an almost uncontrollable itch, then she could go no farther.

"Stand back from the field, Miss Day." The voice was thin, reedy, wheezy, tentative, as if it belonged to something small and wimpy. Day looked around to see from where it had come, but the room still appeared empty. A speaker, then. She stayed where she was. "Move away from the field, Miss Day," it said again. "You obviously know by now that you cannot get through it so you may as well move back and sit down. Unless you prefer to itch continuously."

"Who are you and who are you talking to?" Day said in a loud voice. "I'm the only one here and if you think my name is Day your brain trust has been beating up the wrong person."

"Sit down and be quiet," the voice said in a tone that indicated its owner was accustomed to being obeyed. Day shrugged and sat on a large cushion that lay on the thickly carpeted floor a short distance away from the force field. "Good."

"How about turning up the heat in this place?" Day said. "Since you insist on parading me around the place buck naked, the least you could do is keep me warm." A panel she hadn't noticed before opened on the wall to her left and revealed a fireplace behind it. It lit. "Thanks," she said.

The force field around the divan begin to swirl as if it were a pond into which a pebble had been dropped and, almost like a curtain parting across a stage, it appeared to open, revealing a large, ugly creature the origin of which Day couldn't identify lounging on the divan. It was a neat trick.

"That's a neat trick," Day said. The creature waved one of its arms absently.

"That's all it is, Miss Day. A trick. A mere bending of light and the projection of a static scene to cover my presence until I am ready to show myself. Technology, properly used."

"Yeah, well, you may be a technical whiz but you don't even know who I am. You keep calling me 'Miss Day'."

The creature sighed. "Come, come, Miss Day. You're not dealing with amateurs here. We know exactly who you are and why you're here. What do you think I am, a fool?"

Day shrugged and looked uninterested. "I don't take you for anything. I don't even know you. I do know that from what I've seen so far it's safe to assume you're a barbarian and a clown, if not some kind of nut." She paused to let the insults sink in. "But I have business with you. Assuming you're the thing known as Makteer."

The creature smiled thinly, the only smile possible with those lips. "Indeed." He reached for something long and sharp on the table next to where he lounged, began picking his brown teeth. "Vanday Makteer, at your service."

"Really?" She stood up and approached the force field once more. "The name's Farm, and if you're really at my service I want some clothes, some food, and a door handle I can use to get out of here." She stopped just short of the field and stood there, her eyes staring straight into the Trader's, trying to bore right through him with her glare.

He gazed back tranquilly. "You think you're tough," he remarked matter-of-factly, "But you bruise like any other human."

"You'd bruise too if you had those sloping forehead people working you over. Care to find out?" Makteer laughed and Day's blood felt like it was going to clot. It was a cold laugh, a merciless laugh. Perhaps not an evil laugh, but the laugh of a powerful person who didn't seem concerned by societal constraints, who felt omnipotent in his own sphere of influence.

And Day was smack dab in the heart of his sphere of influence...

"Perhaps I will someday," Makteer replied mildly, "But not today." He finished picking his teeth and put away the implement. "Now, to business. You might as well sit down again; this may take a while." Day wondered what was coming, but knew that whatever it would be, it undoubtedly wouldn't be pleasant. "You are Bonnie Day," Makteer continued, leaning forward for emphasis. "You are known to the organization you call The Club as Supra Nine and you are trying to find the ambassadors from Ramallah and Bolingnar."

"As I said before, my name is Becky Farm and I won a shuttle from one of your minions on Gault. I brought it here to sell it back to you so I can make some money on the deal. I have no idea who this Bonnie Day is you're talking about."

Makteer's face clouded. "Shut up!" he screamed, his voice reaching such a high, piercing pitch that it caused Day to wince. The Trader leaned toward her until his nose almost touched the field separating them. "I told you not to play me for a fool. But since you persist, and since I don't have time for meaningless drivel, perhaps a little demonstration would help." He reached behind himself and touched something. The wall behind him lit with a picture of her, surrounded by more facts about her than she thought anyone besides Auntie could have known.

Day didn't bother wondering how he'd gotten it. But her Becky Farm pretense, at best a long shot in the first place, now seemed stupid and trivial. "Okay. Well if you're so smart then you must also know how good I am. So why don't you give up now and let's keep this short and sweet and painless for you?"

Makteer's eyes widened at the audacity, and his mouth curled into a slight smile. He settled more comfortably onto the divan. "I'll keep it in mind," he replied quietly. "I must admit to a certain amazement that you apparently think you can march in and defeat me all by yourself."

"You have my record. The bigger they are…" she said nonchalantly.

"Indeed? And you really class me with anyone else you've dealt with? We'll have to see about that." He paused and took a smoke from a box on the table beside him, lit it and blew a casual smoke ring. It reached the field and spread outward. "Now, then, enough of this prattle. To business."

"About time," Day said. "Now about those ambassadors..."

Makteer waved his arm, dismissing them. "They are of no importance. They were merely a means to an end."

Day felt a cold lump in her guts. "You mean they're dead."

"Oh, no, not dead. They are quite alive and well, as a matter of fact, and safe here in my castle." The lump started to warm. "I don't kill unnecessarily. I am not a barbarian."

"I beg to differ. How do you explain all those people aboard the QUEEN VICTORIA then? Accident victims?"

"Of course not," Makteer replied. "Those were necessary in order for me to accomplish my goal. I needed to test my technology and my plan."

"You like new technology?"

"Indeed. It can help me get what I want. My space drive, you'll notice, which allows me to exit hyperspace in closer proximity to my prey than any other engine, makes my forces able to mount a sneak attack in space. Where before a ship's sensors would give prior warning of my arrival. I'm quite proud of that little wrinkle on modern propulsion."

"Yeah, nice trick."

"I wish I could take complete credit for it, but it's an invention of a good friend and long time associate. No, the QUEEN VICTORIA episode was merely a dry run, a test toward completion of my overall plan."

"Which is?" Makteer shifted around on the divan, got into a more comfortable position.

"Miss Day, you probably think I'm a rich person." He didn't wait for a comment, but continued "And I suppose I am, by the standards of those lower on the food chain, as it were. And by the standards of the planet I was born on I would be considered particularly well off."

"You were born?"

Makteer looked at her disdainfully. "I was born, Miss Day," he said. "I was spawned on the streets of Rambana Four during what they called the times of confusion there. Are you familiar with the planet?" Day shook her head. She'd heard of the place, and knew that it was anything but the center of the Co-operative, but she'd never been there and didn't know a lot about it. "It was and is one of the poorest areas in this so-called Co-operative. My parents were killed in the food riots when I was three and from then on I lived in the streets. Survival was always difficult, but I discovered that I am blessed with a fine brain and the drive to make a better life for myself. I used both to get off the streets, then off Rambana Four. By the time I was fifteen I was in business, buying and selling workers for the outer colonies."

"You were a slave trader," Day said coldly. "You must be so proud."

Makteer inclined his head slightly in acknowledgement. "Many people called it that name, and thought it evil. But I saw it as a chance to take hopeless wretches and give them a better opportunity somewhere else..."

"...at the point of a blaster," Day added.

"You argue semantics. Anyway, that got me started but after a couple of years I was ready for better things."

"Better for who?"

"Why, me, of course. Eventually, through hard work and acumen, I built my empire."

"And how many bodies did you step over on the way up?"

"Only those that got in my way."

Day shivered. "Don't people mean anything to you at all, Makteer?"

Makteer snorted. "People? People are cheap. You can buy them almost anywhere." He waved his hand and blew another smoke ring. "Besides, many of my associates over the years have found they could improve their own fortunes by tying theirs to mine. Many are still with me."

"You're a real humanitarian," Day said. "I'll bet you have a plaque on your bedroom wall telling you what a wonderful person you are." Makteer's face took on a deep scowl. "This has gone on long enough, Day. This conversation is pointless." He reached behind him again and pressed a button. "I'd like to say it's been pleasant meeting you, but that would be untrue."

The door through which Day had been put into the hall opened and the same thugs who had roughed her up came in. Two had blasters aimed at her. All five were equipped with long metal clubs. "Until later, Miss Day," Makteer said and the force field closed over his image again like a theatrical curtain coming down to end a performance.

Day was ushered out of the room and marched to another blank-walled stone room. This one contained a large, open space in the middle, occupied by a rack-like contraption, a structure to which various wires and straps were attached. Day didn't like the look of it. Then the men started in on her again, beating her with the metal clubs. They started at her feet, smashing them and making her fall to the floor. She tried to curl up, to protect herself, but there was no relief to be had. Her tormentors worked their way over her body, pounding her over and over again until she could do nothing but give in and allow the blackness of unconsciousness to enfold her.

Life returned eventually, slowly. Day could hardly move, and because of the pain she didn't want to. But she did manage to open her eyes and look around, then with a groan, she closed them again.

She hung, spread-eagled, from the rack she'd seen upon entering the room. Thongs suspended her above the floor and dug into her flesh as gravity tried to drag her down. Wires were clipped onto her flesh at strategic points, extending from each finger tip and biting into the skin of her earlobes, nose, sides, and toes. A larger clip held wires firmly to her upper teeth. In front of her, her chief tormentor stood with his hand resting lazily on a control panel, an evil smile on his ugly face.

"You know, missy," he said. "This is gonna be fun." Then he snapped to attention as the door opened and Makteer came in. He stayed at attention as the Trader crossed over to Day and stopped before her.

"An interesting device, this," he said quietly, his eyes gleaming. "It inflicts a great deal of pain, but it does little damage. That way, depending on the setting, I can prolong your agony for hours, days, or even weeks, before the damage becomes severe enough to be permanent."

One of the guards stood across from her, mouth open in a drooling, anticipatory leer. She turned her attention back to Makteer.

"I propose giving you a medium dosage, dragging your eventual death out for at least a week. Then, to prevent meddling like yours in the future, I will ship your body back to your so-called Auntie, where examination of the cadaver will show exactly the conditions under which you died. Does that interest you?"

"Wait a minute, Makteer!" Day pleaded, wearily. "Can't we cut a deal?"

Makteer smiled knowingly. "So you can stab me in the back at a later date? I think not."

"No wait," Day cried desperately. "I can be a real asset to you. You say you're planning something big. I can help."

"You'd switch allegiances just like that?" Makteer snapped his fingers. There was a dry chuckle in his voice. Quickly, desperately, she told him how she'd gotten dragged back into the Club. She admitted her past, her record, and as quickly as ideas would come into her head she outlined ways her skills could benefit Makteer and his organization. She was clutching at straws and knew it, but all she had left otherwise was a long and painful death.

Makteer appeared to consider it for a moment, then said, "I'm sorry, Miss Day, but you're more use to me dead. You'll make a fine example." He turned and headed toward the door. "Go ahead with the procedure."

"Wait," Day screamed. "You're making a big mistake!" Then the door closed with a muffled thud and the next thing she knew was the fires of hell. She screamed again, louder, as pain flooded into her body from the wires, the straps holding her tightly to the rack preventing her from convulsing, from curling into the fetal ball she wanted to be in.

It went on and on like that, a long blast of torture tearing into her body and right through her soul, sending her into unspeakable spasms of agony. Then would come a short respite during which the pain would stop, but she would whimper in agony like some animal pleading to be released from a deadly trap. She had no idea how long the torture went on. It could have been hours, days, or lifetimes. It seemed like the breaks got shorter and shorter, as she got weaker and weaker, as her resolve gradually dissolved and she gave in to the pain, waiting for the blessing of death to release her. She relished the thought that soon her body would let go and she could sleep at last. She hoped it would come soon. But the pain continued, the breaks seemed ever shorter. Finally, she managed to stop her quiet whimpering long enough to summon the strength to beg for mercy. She begged for her life, and she meant it.

Her tormentor grinned back and stabbed at the button again.

Eventually blessed blackness did overtake Day and she gave into it gladly, grateful for the burden of life to be lifted from her at last.

# INTO THE VOID -- Chapter 16

A sensation of floating. Falling. Continuously falling, as if down an endless tunnel or bottomless pit, if such a thing were possible. Except that there was no rush of atmosphere passing by her, no sound coming from her screaming lips. It was just one long, eternally long, fall, an unidentified planet below seemingly rushing up to meet her. Then it was a patchwork quilt of farming fields growing larger in her view, and as she got lower she could make out buildings, vehicles, and finally, when she was getting close enough to almost smell the manure in the fields, she could make out animals and people.

When she had only about a thousand meters to plummet before pounding into the ground, she saw someone below her look up and point in her direction. She opened her mouth to yell for help, but nothing came out and the sudden rush of air almost choked her. She dropped.

Then Bonnie Day bounced and found herself awake and sitting up on a hydraulic bed, bathed in the coldest and clammiest sweat she could remember.

She could remember! That was a good sign.

Then she remembered, and put her head into her hands, sobbing as the memories flooded back into her. She ached unbelievably, in every part of her being. It was as if she'd been torn into little pieces and reassembled by a taxidermist, her barely living shell stitched together and stretched over a synthetic soul.

She knew she was Bonnie Day, but what did that mean? She shook her head to clear it. What was going on? She was supposed to be dead. She'd wanted to be dead.

She'd been dead, as far as she'd been concerned.

There was a toilet on one wall of the metal room in which she found herself, with a washbasin next to it and a mirror on the wall over the basin. Day got up and went to the mirror. A puffy, bruised and battered face looked back, one she scarcely recognized. Then she was leaning forward and vomiting into the sink, retching madly and automatically as the spasms took control of her, wracking her with heaves that came so violently she could barely breathe between them. She dropped to her knees and slid sideways until her head was cupped in her hands over the toilet bowl.

When the spasms subsided, she wiped her mouth with her hand and, exhausted, lay on the floor next to the toilet. In seconds she'd returned to blackness.

In bed again, the floating sensation from the liquid-filled mattress providing her with a soothing, lulling feeling. What?

She sat up and swung her legs off the mattress, then gingerly stepped onto the floor and went back over to the sink, carefully avoiding making eye contact with herself in the mirror. She turned on the faucet and gave her face a gentle wash, with a liberal amount of soap applied gingerly to her battered flesh. She toweled herself dry carefully and decided to take another look at the damage.

She was no longer naked, but rather dressed in the nondescript coverall worn while shipboard by uncounted legions of spacers. It was gray, and lacked insignia or other identity marks. It did, however, give her a clue that, combined with the appearance of the little metal cell in which she found herself, told her she was aboard a spaceship. She wriggled out of the coverall and took inventory.

Makteer's thugs had been careful not to break anything, physically. Other than that they'd had a field day. She was bruised like she'd never seen before, like she'd been trampled by a herd of hoofed animals or dragged behind a ground car. Day went back to the mirror and looked at her face while gingerly feeling around her skull. The working over was vicious to the eye, but had left little compromised structurally. She suspected most of the real harm had been done to her in non-physical ways that would take longer to heal.

Makteer probably had a great business going in those pain machines...

But lighten up! She was alive, and reasonably healthy! She dressed, then ran her fingers through her hair in a simplistic attempt to comb the rat's nest. It helped a bit, as much for her spirits as for her appearance.

A "Bong!" sounded from somewhere overhead and she turned away from the mirror. The door opened to reveal a small, dainty-looking woman in the corridor outside. She was dressed like a nurse, and she smiled cheerfully as she came into the room. The door slid shut behind her with a hissing noise, closing with a heavy metal thud.

"Well, and how are we today?" the woman asked pleasantly, professionally.

Day looked her over and decided she was either an excellent actress, or the real item. "Judging by the way I look and feel, I'd say I've been lots better," she volunteered, a slight smile turning up the corners of her mouth. "But I can't answer for how you are."

The ludicrousness of the situation struck her, the primly starched "nurse-compatible" showing up at what was obviously the brig, acting as if everything were completely normal. Day wondered if the woman knew how she'd gotten into the condition in which she found her and, if so, why the act? "Where are we?"

"Why, you're a guest on the Trader's personal flagship, you silly person. Didn't you bother looking where you were going when you came aboard?"

"I was busy. Where are we going?"

"Now, aren't you just full of questions? I really don't know where we're going; that's not the sort of thing I'm told. My duties are to help make sure everyone stays healthy, and that means right now you're under my care. So tell me, how did you get into this awful condition?"

"You really don't know?"

"Why would I ask if I knew?"

Day decided to give her the benefit of the doubt. If nothing else, she was a reasonably friendly face in a place where Day didn't anticipate finding too many. "It's not important. Let's just say I had a bit of an accident."

The woman frowned and pursed her lips. "Well, okay, but you'd better take care of yourself. I had the devil of a time tending to you. You seemed so badly hurt."

"Thank you."

"Think nothing of it. Now that you're starting to feel better, is there anything I can get you?"

"Some breakfast, maybe?"

The nurse shook her head. "It's too late for breakfast and lunch." She pouted. "You would have to ask for the one thing I'm not allowed to bring you. Food. Trader Makteer specifically told me to take care of you and see to your needs, but not to feed you because he's planning to have you for dinner tonight."

Day started at the thought of Makteer having her for dinner, not knowing to what sort of victuals his race might be partial, then smiled inwardly at the silliness of the thought. Makteer wouldn't have let her live just to dine on her later.

"And when might that be? I'm hungry."

The nurse checked her watch ring. "In about an hour. Think you can hang on that long?"

"I have a choice? I'll manage, thanks. And thanks for taking care of me."

"I do hope you enjoy your cruise." She pulled a remote control from a pocket and pressed a button on it. The door slid open again. "Well, I'd better run along and see to the rest of my duties. Just holler if you need anything."

"How? Set the bedclothes on fire and send up smoke signals?"

The nurse laughed. "See? You're feeling better. No, just call out. I'll get your message." She turned and went through the opening. "Take care of yourself, now. You hear?" Day nodded and the door slid shut again.

Bugs. What a surprise. Well, she had an hour to kill, it seemed, before someone brought her back to see Makteer and she found out what was going on. She decided to do what she could to spruce up and went over to the sink and got to work.

She was reasonably presentable by the time the next "Bong!" came, thanks to some good, old fashioned – albeit gentle – scrubbing. She was lounging on the bed when the sound came, and swung her legs over the edge and sat up, facing where the door would open. When it did, it revealed a gigantic human, one of the largest examples she'd ever seen. He was unarmed, except for his own appendages, and was so big he could scarcely fit through the little doorway. His face was pockmarked and scarred as if he'd had a field day popping pimples as a youth, and he had but one eyebrow extending across the width of his forehead, almost joining his wildly unkempt hair. Day thought he looked like he'd just swung out of a tree and wondered if, when he put his arms down, his knuckles would scrape the deck. To complete the image, he was wearing a shirt with Gargantua holo'd across it. Day expected tattoos as well, though none were in evidence.

She finished her once over, then slid her feet casually to the deck and stood up. "I suppose you've come to escort me to my dinner date?" The man nodded, but said nothing and motioned her into the corridor. She squeezed through the space between the doorway and "Gargantua," and stopped. "Which way?" He picked her up, turned her 180 degrees, and set her down, then gave her what was probably to him a gentle push, but which almost sent Day sprawling on the metal deck. "Okay, okay," she said, miffed, "You could just point, you know." He shoved her again. She took the hint and started walking.

She quickly became impressed with Makteer's "yacht." It would put many liners to shame and its fixtures made her lovely Xannyk look positively entry level. Heck, even the imaginary yacht she'd invented as her cover story for Stornoway would pale next to this. The corridors themselves were generic spaceship, though finely carpeted and with tapestries displayed in abundance on the bulkheads, but they, and the occasional glimpse of open rooms they passed, told her that she and Makteer had at least one thing in common: a penchant for going first class.

She also spent the trip memorizing the positions of places and items she thought could come in handy, such as spacesuit closets, storerooms, weapons cabinets. It never hurt to be prepared.

Each time they reached intersecting corridors, she would receive another of the none-too-gentle touches from her escort, indicating in which direction she should go. She finally found herself facing a closed door on which was stenciled "Control Room. Authorized Personnel Only." She stopped, and her escort nearly trampled onto her heels. He growled unpleasantly and put one big arm on her shoulder, holding her. He reached around her with his other arm and pressed a red button beside the door. It shushed open, revealing Makteer and what Day assumed was his inner circle. Makteer was sitting in a lounger in the middle of the room, the others huddled around him. A few of his hangers on looked up as the door opened, giving Day a disinterested glance before turning their attention back to their boss. It looked like a council of war.

Day was pushed from behind again and practically fell into the control room. Gathering what dignity she could, which wasn't much, she moved away from the big oaf and approached the gathering. Makteer looked up and smiled thinly. There was no warmth in the smile.

"Well, look what Gargantua brought in," he said. "Good evening, Miz Day. I trust you had a pleasant sleep?"

"It was a little shorter than I'd expected," she replied, "But other than that it was fine. Nice ship."

"Thank you. I have nice everything. Thank you, Gargantua, you may leave." Day's escort saluted clumsily, turned, and left, the door closing behind him. "A most able assistant," Makteer said. "Mute since an unfortunate accident earlier in his - ah - association with me, which at least keeps him from talking back, but with unquestionable loyalty and great strength and stamina. An earlier - volunteer - for my pain device, in fact. He'd have made a good member of your Club." Day let the comment pass without replying. She wanted two things from Makteer right then: food and information.

"I was told I was being invited to dinner."

"And so you were. It should be served presently. You'll forgive me if I have arranged for our meal to be served here; we're in the middle of a meeting. Which brings me to the next subject. Why you're here."

"Yeah. I thought you'd decided to dispense with my services."

"I changed my mind."

"Well I hope you got one that works this time." She regretted it as soon as she'd said it; Makteer's inner sanctum was hardly the place to start poking at fate with a pointy stick. Makteer, however, chose to ignore the barb.

"I thought you might be of use. As you so eloquently pointed out at our last meeting, I believe it was while you begged for your miserable life, you have a lot to offer. I don't yet know what it is that you can do for me, but it seemed a reasonable course of action to keep you handy until that function becomes obvious. Or until I tire of waiting. You can do nothing to harm me. Ah, here's the food."

The door had slid open again and a line of stewards came in, pushing antigrav dollies loaded with covered trays. A heavenly smell began to wash over Day and, much to her dismay and embarrassment, her mouth began to water uncontrollably.

"I see the Pavlovian aspect of our relationship has already begun to take effect," Makteer said. "Good." He stood up and walked over to the first tray, lifting the cover to reveal a huge, steaming pile of some rice-like dish. "Perhaps you should have the first helping after me, Miz Day. Eat well."

The covers were off the other trays by then and he walked around the dollies, pointing at various dishes. They were spooned onto a plate for him as he went back to his lounger, sat, and pressed a button on it. A little tabletop tray slid out of one side and positioned itself in front of him. A steward brought Makteer's bulging plate to him and set it in front of him, then laid out utensils. "Now the rest of you may begin."

There was no discussion during dinner; the fifteen or so people in the room occupied themselves with the business of sustenance,

Day in particular digging in with gusto to one of the better meals she'd had in the recent past. She had to admit that Makteer knew how to live; at least her house arrest wouldn't be too unpleasant.

When everyone had finished, Makteer clapped his hands and the remnants of the meal were whisked away. Then he ordered a holographic projector set up, and soon afterward it was wheeled in by Gargantua, who set it up and flicked the switch. A three dimensional logo "TVM Enterprises" appeared, floating in the space above it.

"Dim the lights, please." said Makteer. An underling complied and the holoprojection positively leaped out of the air at the onlookers. "Now. We've had a nice meal, it's time for business. Some of you are probably wondering what we're doing out here and where we're going. It's time to outline my plan." He flicked his wrist and the hologram disappeared. He turned to a creature near him, one wearing a pseudo military uniform. "Bring the other ship captains into the loop, please."

The officer went over to a panel and pressed a button. "Attention!"

"As most of you know, I am the greatest of the Traders. I buy and sell and amass things, and so far have managed to become one of the most powerful, influential Traders operating today." He flicked his wrist again and a new holographic image floated above the projector: one of a silver-haired, kindly looking old man with strong, firm features, but a gentle twinkle in his eye. Day thought he looked like he'd have made a good grandfather, despite the hint of steel behind that gentle twinkle. "But this man's empire makes mine look puny in comparison, and that cannot be allowed." He motioned toward the floating head. "I speak, of course, of the Shameer of Shammarrah, whose image floats before us." Makteer spoke the man's name in a tone of both awe and distaste, as if the man were somehow both a god and a devil, and not merely a corporate adversary. "This man," he continued, "is the envy of all who, like me, live to acquire. That envy will soon be of me. Next image."

The hologram changed to show a fleet of ships in space, mostly small craft deployed in a rough semi-circle surrounding a much larger vessel. "This is my armada, as it currently heads toward the Shameer's fleet, and this is what I propose to do."

Makteer rose from his seat and went over to the projection, started circling it as he spoke. He ordered up the next hologram, of a slightly larger, but more ragged fleet of ships. "My opponent is currently on Bunquerill, his home world and base. From there, this slimy creature thumbs his nose at my empire. And for that, he must pay.

"Even as we speak, his ships are taking his daughter to Oxford Four, where he has enrolled her in the University. She will not make it." A series of gasps could be heard around the room. Makteer shook his head at the reaction. "I have no malice toward this child," he said. "It is her father who is my adversary, and for that I have our plan prepared. Remember those two pompous asses we have in safekeeping on Taddayoosh, those backward ambassadors? That is what we will do to the Shameer's girl."

The pieces finally fell into place for Day. Makteer had said the ambassadors' kidnapping was merely a dry run; he was going to grab the Shameer's daughter and use her for leverage. She shook her head. He was enough to give capitalism a bad name!

She stood up. "You're going to destroy the Shameer's fleet and kill all those people just so you can prove a point. Nice."

Makteer angled his head as if he were royalty receiving plaudits from the masses. "Thank you. I thought you could appreciate such nuance, but even you don't get it. I don't want to, as you say, make a point with the Shameer. I want the Shameer. For years I have looked on his empire from afar, biding my time until I could make it mine and become the greatest Trader. Now is that time!" He began laughing, a loud, abrasive cackle that made Day realize he was as insane as his lunatic scheme.

He was also, she realized, fully capable of pulling it off...

# PUSH COMES TO SHOVE
## -- Chapter 17

Bonnie Day's inner alarm clock woke her in the wee hours of the morning. Without sitting up, she took a few seconds to flush the sleep from her body then put her plan, such as it was, into action. She curled into fetal position and started moaning, the noises increasing in intensity for the benefit of whoever was listening.

After a few minutes of that, the lights came on and she threw her arm over her eyes as if the brightness were painful to her. She got up and stumbled over to the basin and pretended to be violently ill, over and over again. Finally, she collapsed onto the deck and lay there.

She heard the door slide open and the soft patter of a single pair of feet coming toward her. The door closed with a thunk.

"My goodness me," said a voice Day recognized as the nurse who'd ministered to her earlier, "What's going on here?" Day grabbed her stomach and doubled up on the floor. The nurse tut tutted and reached down to touch her forehead.

Then Day's foot shot out and up, striking the nurse on the side of her head as she bent over. Her eyes widened with disbelief as her head was forced upward and backward. The blow staggered her just long enough for Day to leap to her feet and, using a sideways chop with the back of her hand, send the nurse sprawling to the floor, unconscious. Day undressed her quickly, then wriggled out of her own coverall. She donned the nurse's uniform, noticing happily that the remote control for the cell door was still in a pocket.

She grabbed the coverall she'd chucked and tore strips from it, fashioning some makeshift bonds. The nurse moaned softly. "Just stay out a few more minutes," Day grunted, softly enough that the hidden microphones shouldn't pick it up. "I don't want to have to hurt you any more."

She bound her, tying her hands and feet tightly enough to prevent escape, but not so tightly as to require an amputation afterward. Tearing a wider strip from the coverall, Day fashioned a gag, then tore up the remainder of the coverall and stuffed the strips into her pocket. The job done, she stood up and smoothed out the nurse's uniform, then went back to the mirror and tried to make herself look as believable as possible. Then she pulled out the remote control and opened the door.

In moments she stood, unopposed, outside the control room door. She hadn't met anyone, undoubtedly because of the hour and the lack of an alarm so far. She opened the door and went in. The officer of the watch turned boredly, saw only the uniform, and waved her in. He went back to his displays. Day thanked whatever lucky stars there may have been for lack of conscious thought on the part of the crewman. She stole up behind the man and gave him a quick chop on the side of his neck. There was a muffled exhalation of breath and he slid to one side. Day pushed him from the chair and dragged him to the corner of the room, away from the door. She trussed him up and gagged him and went back to his station.

She slid into the pilot's seat and took inventory. It was standard stuff, and she quickly located the communications console and turned it on. Then she stopped in her tracks. Who could she contact? She could read their heading on the screen, but that didn't mean anything because they could have been going toward a Jump point, after which they could change course in a multitude of ways. Or they may have just come out of a Jump recently while she was indisposed. That made warning the Shameer's fleet like trying to hit a star in the next galaxy with a hand blaster. Even if she knew where it was. A blanket message, sent out in all directions, would only guarantee her bid at heroics would be cut short when all the ships surrounding them picked it up.

But maybe if she could squirt a quick alert to Auntie and the gang..."

It would be a difficult roundabout way to send a warning, and she'd probably only get one chance. She tapped a message into the comsole, included the current position and heading of the ship according to its instruments, a time stamp and a quick status report. She coded it, called up the coordinates for Gault and compiled it into a microsecond burst. Her fingers positively flew over the keyboard. All that remained was to send it and head for the escape pods.

"Get your hands away from that console and stand up!" Day put her hands over her head and got out of the chair. She turned to face her visitor, who stood just inside the doorway, covering her with a blaster. From her uniform, it appeared she was the next officer of the watch. Day had had the misfortune of timing her attack at watch change! "That's good. Now don't move a muscle or you're dead."

"You don't really want to fire that thing in here, do you?" Day replied sweetly. "It wouldn't do a lot of good to all that fancy equipment, you know."

"Shut up." The woman kept Day covered while she went to the comm panel on the bulkhead. "Security to control room. We have an intruder." She turned her full attention back to Day. "Now move away from that equipment and come into the open. Now." Day shrugged and started to comply. She stubbed her toe on the edge of the chair's pedestal as she got up. She cried out in pain and, reflexively, reached down to her foot, her hand slapping roughly and painfully against the control panel as she did it.

"Get away from that equipment before you blunder into something important."

Day limped into the middle of the room and stood there on one foot, massaging her other one with her fingers. Footsteps sounded in the corridor and a group of armed security people burst through the doorway and surrounded her. Day put down her foot and held her hands over her head again. The group stood uneasily for an interminable few seconds during which Day smiled innocently and her captors glared back at her. They were obviously waiting for someone to make a decision, and there didn't appear to be one among them who'd take the responsibility.

The interlude didn't last long.

"Well, Miss Day," said Makteer as he entered the control room, "it looks as if I should have had you destroyed while I had the chance." He walked toward her, the circle of guards parting for him as if he were somehow carrying an opposite magnetic charge, and faced Day. She shrugged, as well as she could with her hands over her head. "Fortunately, it's not too late."

"I wouldn't count on that, Makteer."

"I would." He came close and leaned in to her face, his expression tightening into an ugly snarl. "You forget who runs things here." He slapped her roughly, a stinging blow that caught Day by surprise. Her face recoiled from the attack and a red mark began forming where he'd struck her. Then she locked her stare onto his, her expression filling with steely resolve.

"Are fists the only thing you understand when it gets down to it, Makteer?"

The Trader's demeanor softened somewhat. "Not at all. I have access to whatever means I choose." Then he smiled, coldly. "But sometimes I choose to hit. You might be surprised how effective it can be."

Makteer took a step back. He looked around for the officer of the watch and motioned her forward. "Get to your station and see to your business." He turned his attention to the guards. "See that she doesn't bother me any more."

Day was led from the control room surrounded by the security detail and marched swiftly back in the direction from which she'd come. When they arrived back at her room, other crewmembers were just removing the nurse. The woman gave Day a withering expression. As they met, Day apologized to the woman, but her words were ignored. Then she was shoved roughly through the doorway and sprawled onto the deck. The guards never lowered their blasters. Before they left her there, they searched her clothing and retrieved the remote control for the door.

They didn't lock her in this time, though. One guard remained in the room with her, blaster at the ready, while another took up a position in the corridor outside, blaster in a similar state of preparedness. For all she knew, they had guards with blasters at intervals all the way back to the control room. Day sat on the bunk and smiled sweetly.

The status quo was maintained through several shift changes, and whoever was giving orders to her watchers had obviously told them not to give her as much as the time of day because any attempt she made to even make small talk was met with stony silence. Day resigned herself to a boring ordeal.

Time dragged on. She estimated that, assuming that room service and the changing of the guard were performed every eight hours, she'd been through about four days. For all she knew, Makteer could have already scooped the Shameer's daughter and they were back on course for Taddayoosh.

It would have been nice to at least have a video to watch...

Makteer rubbed his hands together in anticipation and looked at the chronometer on the control panel: five minutes until first contact with the Shameer's fleet. The atmosphere was positively electric. The crew, well oiled and chomping at the bit, was going through checklists, making sure everything would go according to plan when the fleet jumped out of hyperspace. Navigation systems, intra fleet communications, weaponry, all received thumbs up.

Makteer's smile broadened. He looked at his watch ring. Two minutes!

The countdown proceeded normally, with the final weapons check completed at J Minus 30 seconds. His crew tensed, waiting for the other shoe to drop. Makteer leaned over the shoulder of the Admiral and close to his ear. "Now it begins." The officer nodded calmly.

Then came that flip-flop of the guts that signaled the hyperspace Jump and everything went fuzzy for a moment. Makteer involuntarily grabbed for the support of the Admiral's armrest as his knees wobbled under him. Then it was over and he had that thickness of tongue that followed the bending of the Relativity rules. "Thtatus check," he mumbled with difficulty.

It took a few seconds for the rest of the personnel to find their voices after the Jump, then the reports started coming in.

"Ship secure."

"Traffic ahead!"

"Fleet communications re-established." And so on down the line. Makteer was beginning to feel very good.

"Status of traffic?"

"Five ships, sir, just where they should be and looking like they should."

"Good. Carry on with the operation, Admiral." He let go the armrest and stretched himself up to his full height.

"Right, sir. Communications, patch me through to the fleet, secure channel."

"Ready."

"This is Control. Prepare for engagement." He peered at a screen in front of him, "Attack plan alpha. Turn left fourteen degrees, down twenty three." He motioned the comm officer to cut the channel, then turned to his navigator. "Niće job, Mike. You hit the nail on the head better than I could have hoped."

"Aye, sir." The officer turned to acknowledge the compliment, then bent back over her computers. After a few seconds she said "We'll be in range in one minute."

"Weapons, bring the dishes to bear on any ship but the flagship. Proceed with Phase One."

Doors opened in the hulls of the leading ships, and parabolic dishes rolled out into position. They tracked across space until they were aimed at the Shameer's ships, then they locked into place. On Makteer's bridge, a series of "Readys" was heard through the speakers.

"All ships in position and ready for engagement, sir," the Admiral heard. He nodded. "Go ahead, mister." The weapons officer began a countdown from fifteen seconds. When he reached zero, he stabbed at a button in front of him, and four other fingers on the other four lead ships stabbed in unison with his.

The disrupter dishes on the ships lit up angrily and belched a stabbing blade of bright blue horror at each of the Shameer's ships, tearing a hole in the hull of each. Atmosphere and debris were blown into space.

"Analyze debris," ordered Makteer.

"Metal and fabric, plastics," came the reply. Then, a few seconds later. "That's it. No bodies, sir."

Makteer ran his hand through where his hair would have been. Damn that Shameer's eyes! So oblivious and overconfident that he ran his ships on automatic control with no armed escort!

Maybe he didn't like paying pilots...

"Sir?" Makteer realized the Admiral was waiting for his instructions. He turned back to the job at hand. "Er, proceed, Admiral. The Shameer is obviously not expecting company."

"Aye sir." The Admiral was patched through the fleet again. "Proceed with Phase Two. Boarding teams, go." Farther aft, and repeated in the accompanying spacecraft, airlocks trundled open and Makteer's army of black space suited soldiers spewed into the void. They began crossing the short distance between the fleets.

Bonnie Day looked up at the speaker in the ceiling when she heard the boarding team sent on its way, and her mood got darker. She glared at the guard facing her, blaster held ready as always.

Outside, the various parts of the black suited army were joining, forming a gigantic sphere to surround the Shameer's fleet. On his ship, Makteer was smiling happily. It would all be over in a few minutes and the Shameer hadn't even offered a fight! Makteer moved closer to the viewscreen to get a better view.

Then his jaw dropped open and he gurgled inanely as row upon row of figures began issuing from the Shameer's ships, armed with blaster rifles! Some of Makteer's soldiers were shot and began floating lifelessly. Some of the Shameer's people carried larger, two person weapons and from the direction they were rocketing their intention was obvious...

"Admiral, turn those dishes on those people," Makteer shouted. The Admiral barked a series of orders and the disrupters began to swing slowly toward their new targets. But it was too late. The big, two-person blasters tore the dishes apart before they could do any more damage. Then the weapons were turned on Makteer's ships themselves, while some of their compatriots bunched around them in defensive positions.

Makteer's soldiers fought back, and took their toll, but they hadn't expected to be met outside, on equal terms. The advance was stopped and the vacuum between the flotillas became littered with wildly spinning or aimlessly meandering bodies from both sides.

The Shameer's blaster cannon assault continued, tearing pieces from Makteer's armada. Ships shuddered violently at the rending of the beams and bits of vessel were torn away and floated away into space. On board, compartments lost their atmosphere and were sealed off by airtight bulkheads.

Aft, Bonnie Day heard and felt the commotion and stopped her navel gazing. She looked up at the nearest guard, who suddenly looked a lot younger than he had a few moments before. "Sounds like your boss may have bitten off more than he can chew," she remarked conversationally. The guard looked around uncertainly, his eyes meeting those of his companion outside, then both of them shifted their gaze nervously to the deck.

The ship shuddered and the outer guard swayed. Overhead, the intercom hooted for attention and a voice called "All hands, battle stations! All hands, battle stations! Prepare for attempted boarding!" The guards' eyes met again and it was obvious they had no idea what to do.

Supra 9, however, did. "So what'll it be, guys? Stay here and die with me or go and fight for your lives? I think your boss has more pressing problems right now than one little girl, eh?" The ship lurched again, violently, and an emergency klaxon started wailing obnoxiously.

The guard outside looked more frightened than he'd probably

thought possible. "What do you think?" he asked his mate. "Should we just lock her in and go help?"

"We'd better check. Call the bridge. I'll keep her covered." He pointed his blaster directly at Day's head. "And no funny stuff." The first guard nodded and went out of view. Day faced the remaining guard.

The ship lurched again and the guard was thrown against the door frame. Day leapt from the bed and attacked. She aimed her first blow at the hand holding the weapon, knocking the blaster to the deck. Then she chopped him on the side of the neck and he followed the blaster, landing beside it in an unconscious heap. Day grabbed the gun and dragged the body out of sight of the doorway, then took up a defensive position just inside the room, waiting for the other guard to return.

She heard him coming and, before he reached the room, barged into the corridor. Startled, he gave Day the split second she needed to shoot the blaster out of his hand. He cried out and looked at her in fear. "Don't hurt me," he said.

"You were all set to hurt me," she pointed out, "But don't worry. I won't kill you unless you make me." She motioned him into the cell. "Now get in there with your buddy. And give me both of your door controls." The guard obeyed, retrieving his buddy's remote and handing them to Day.

Day locked them in and started down the corridor. The ship heaved again and she hit the bulkhead hard with her shoulder. She regained her balance, rubbing the site of the coming bruise, and headed aft to where the life pods should be located. As she ran through the corridors, it appeared to her that Makteer's call to battle stations had deteriorated into complete chaos. People pounded up and down the corridors, holding weapons but not doing anything with them, fright written on their faces. Most of them ran by Day without giving her a glance. A couple must have recognized her, for their eyes widened as they met, but they were bent on being elsewhere and continued on as if she were just another crewmember.

Day made steady progress, though it was slow going because the ship kept lurching and bouncing, throwing her heavily into the bulkheads and, occasionally, right to the deck. But she pressed on. What else was there to do?

Makteer was livid and nearly gibbering inanely at what he saw happening. It didn't take a military genius to know that, while his force may not have been outnumbered, it was certainly outclassed. He was taking a terrible beating.

On the viewscreen, the Trader saw a huge explosion engulf the ship beside his.

"We've lost number three, sir," announced the comm officer, rather superfluously. Makteer whirled on the fleet Admiral.

"What kind of strategy do you call this?"

The officer stared straight ahead calmly. "It's the strategy we developed together, sir. It's what you ordered." That was the wrong thing to say. Makteer took a step toward him, reached into his clothing and pulled out a blaster. What was left of the Admiral hit the deck with a thud. Makteer whirled around to the ship Captain, whose eyes were wide.

"You're in charge of the fleet. See that you do better than him."

The Captain gulped and saluted. "Thank you, sir." He moved toward the control panel. "Prepare to break off the engagement," he ordered, then he saw Makteer's blaster aimed at his head, "Belay that order."

"That's better. Now complete your mission. Then destroy all of those ships except for the lead one. I'll be in my cabin." Makteer turned on his heel and stomped out of the control room, the new Admiral's face filling with relief at the sight. He turned back to his duties.

Day turned left at an intersection she thought should lead outward toward the hull. The shuddering was getting worse, making her careen painfully off bulkheads and dividers. She stepped up her pace as well as she could. The ship lurched again and the sound of tearing metal ahead caused her to pause. An airtight bulkhead slammed into place in front of her, blocking her way.

"That figures." She went back to the crossroads and tried another way, the only path left open. It was the wrong way to the escape pods, though, so she turned back at the first branch that led outward again, but it was blocked around the first curve. Then the ship lurched with a particularly violent movement, a horrible tearing noise, and everything around her went black.

The crimson emergency lights came on almost immediately, giving the ship a frightening, deathly glow and making progress even more difficult. Day picked herself up from the deck and headed back the way she'd come. At one point, the scream of abused space ship apparatus came dangerously close and she leapt forward; then the deck above was on the same level as hers as it came crashing down. She ran, trying to avoid debris. An airtight bulkhead rammed into place behind her.

She skidded to a halt at an all-too-familiar bend in the corridor. The control room was ahead, the front of the ship. The last place she wanted to be! She had to get past it and aft again, to the escape pods on the port side of the ship. She ran forward.

Makteer went directly aft to a place a short distance from the control room. He pressed his hand to an unmarked section of bulkhead and it lit up to reveal the perimeter of what had been until then a hidden door. It opened, and Makteer ducked into the corridor beyond it. He swayed and slammed into the bulkhead as the ship took yet another hit. The bulkhead tore open beside him, leaving the frame of his secret door bowed outward from the pressure on the metal. Makteer ran on.

Outside, the Shameer's soldiers were getting closer to what was left of Makteer's ships. Their heavy, blaster cannons were tearing ever more gaping holes in their opponents' vessels, and many of Makteer's soldiers had surrendered or were trying to retreat in disarray. They found no place to go, though; two of Makteer's ships had already been converted into expanding clouds of gas, dust, and debris.

"Captain, I mean Admiral, this is ridiculous. We've got to get out of here!"

The officer spun around to face his comm officer, from whom the words had issued. "You heard the boss."

"To hell with Makteer. He's going to get us all killed. We've got to save our own skins!" A blaster appeared in his hand and most of the Admiral slumped to the floor. He took over the center seat and patched himself into the intraship circuit. "All hands! Prepare for acceleration in thirty seconds!" He turned to face the glassy, numb expressions of the remaining bridge crew. "We're getting out of here."

Day pounded to a stop, panting, outside the remains of a door that looked like it shouldn't have been there in the first place. On a hunch, she went through it and ran onward down the narrow passageway beyond. She stopped short when it ended abruptly. She was in a small antechamber with a round porthole mounted in the far bulkhead.

An all-too-familiar back was next to the window, apparently poking at a number pad in front of it. The panel surrounding the porthole slid up, revealing a plush little ship on the other side.

"So the rat is deserting his sinking ship, eh?" Day said.

Makteer whirled around, face looking like rage incarnate. "This is your doing!"

Day smiled. "Could be, Makteer. Or maybe you just ran out of luck. It doesn't matter. You're finished."

"Not as long as I breathe," he snarled, and lunged at her. Day sidestepped and Makteer slammed onto the deck where she'd been standing. He rolled over and staggered to his knees, his hand reaching into a pocket.

"Nice little escape pod you've got here, Makteer. Too bad you'll never use it." Day leapt at him, knocking him back to the deck. His hand came out of his pocket and Day saw it held a blaster. She jumped sideways and avoided the blast, then pounced on Makteer and knocked the gun from his hand. It bounced across the deck and came to rest against the far bulkhead. Day wrapped her hands around Makteer's throat and pressed, hard.

Makteer may have been as mean as they come, but he wasn't physically strong. His arms flailed and he tried to buck Day off, but she was trained and she was determined. Makteer gurgled unpleasantly and his eyes rolled up in their sockets. The breath hissed from his lungs and he twitched sickeningly. Day held on a few moments more to make sure the Trader would trade no more, then got up, panting and sweating.

On the bridge, the Admiral ordered power to the main drive. But none came, and he made the only decision he could. "All hands abandon ship" sounded throughout the ship, and what crew was left spilled into the corridors and headed for the escape pods.

Day stuck her head through the opening into Makteer's lifeboat and took a look. It was even smaller than the little shuttle she'd stolen, let alone the Xannyk, but it would do in a pinch. Heck, a space suit would have been fine just then. She withdrew her head and put her right leg over the sill, placing it on the step inside the little ship.

Then she was grabbed from behind and dragged backwards, thrown painfully against the far bulkhead. Dazed, she shook her head and looked up to see Gargantua standing over her, panic and rage on his ugly face. The huge man looked like he would have growled if he could. He pointed to Makteer's body and, in an unmistakably unpleasant gesture, informed Day she was about to join the Trader. Day got to her knees.

"Look," she pleaded, "We're all going to die if we don't get off this ship right away. You can feel it. How long do you think you'll live if you don't get off now?"

The gigantic man paused for a second. Then he lunged at Day with a quickness that took her by surprise and she once again found herself flying through the air. She hit the opposite bulkhead squarely on her back and slid to the deck. "I guess that means you don't study logic," she said weakly.

Gargantua poised to strike again; he leapt, but just then the ship shook violently, so he just missed his planned trajectory. Day avoided his grasp as he passed her and ricocheted off the bulkhead. Then she saw Makteer's blaster, laying beckoning on the deck. She grabbed it and whirled around, leveling Gargantua with a shot that sheared off part of his left side and left the rest of him on the deck, bleeding profusely from a gigantic hole, his eyes bugging out in amazement at the injustice of it all.

"So much for might being right," Day said as she stuck the blaster into her pocket and dove into the lifeboat. She was relieved to find the craft's operation straightforward; she sealed the ship and set it in motion. Seconds later, the view through the porthole showed the outside of Makteer's ship, floating gently away from her as she was shot out into space. She sat down on the overstuffed couch and activated the viewscreen.

Makteer's was the only ship left from his fleet, and from what Day could see it wouldn't last long. Large pieces of it were drifting off into space as if they were little satellites of the Trader's private metal planet. As Day watched, a series of coordinated beams from the Shameer's force tore into the section that housed the power plant, and the ship shuddered once with an almost human gesture of finality before turning into a huge fireball that caused the viewscreen to drop four intensity settings to compensate. Day nodded with satisfaction.

She ordered up a tactical display and took a quick inventory of the space around her. The Shameer's fleet had suffered its share of damage as well, but with the destruction of the last of Makteer's ships his soldiers were heading back to their ships. It also appeared that the main ship was undamaged; she could see defensive forces set up all around it, forces that were now dispersing. It didn't look like many of Makteer's people had stuck around, alive. There were many blips on the screen, but they were for the most part drifting bodies. She scanned the area. The few who still survived seemed to be either trying to get away on their suit thrusters which, given their location in deep space, would be difficult, or surrendering. Those opting for the latter were being led inboard, presumably at gunpoint. All in all, Day thought, a most satisfying scenario. "Computer," she said, "fire up this thing's distress beacon and make sure it's heard." Day pulled her feet up under her on the couch and snuggled deeply into its cushions, waiting.

# MISSION ACCOMPLISHED
## -- Chapter 18

Bonnie Day lounged with her new friend Sharona, in the salon aboard her father's flagship. The wine was excellent, the food even better, and the atmosphere a 180-degree turnaround from that of Makteer's ship. The company was good, too.

"My father and I thank you again for your selfless acts, from the bottom of our hearts," Sharona told her not-for-the-first-or-last time. "If not for your warning..." She raised her wine glass and clinked it with Day's. They drank deeply, again.

Day was beginning to get quite a buzz, and it was only her second glass. She made a mental note to ask for a supply of the stuff to take with her; it might just end up rivaling Scotch as her drink of choice. Or maybe it was just the glow of accomplishment, or of being stroked by a grateful rich person. Whatever. The wine was fine and she wanted more.

She could see why Makteer might have coveted the Shameer's stuff.

"I wasn't sure if my message had even gone out," she said between sips. "As you can imagine, I was under a certain amount of pressure at the time."

The girl nodded solemnly. "I'm glad you handled it. My father's people were understandably surprised to hear from your people, and only had a short time to prepare." She took a deep gulp of the wine and wiped her hand across her mouth. "Fortunately, when you live in our position, you're used to people wanting to knock you down. It becomes second nature to maintain a reasonable state of preparedness." She took another long gulp. "That's not to minimize your work, though, Bonnie. Without that, and a little tactical advice from your people, I'd have been in a great deal of trouble."

Day nodded. From what Sharona had told her, Auntie had been able to put two and two together, and come up with a nice, round four. She had to give Auntie credit; she had brains and sublime organizational and tactical skills. And she had to admit grudgingly that the Club did serve a purpose.

You couldn't let the Makteers have the run of the universe unchecked.

Which reminded her. "I guess the next step is to clean up Taddayoosh, which will require the Co-op going in there in force. If you'll allow me, I'll contact my office again and give them a detailed report. Then I'll meet them there. But I want to get there first; I have a couple things to do, like release those ambassadors. I also want to collect my ship."

But the Shameer's daughter would hear nothing of it. "You have no need to risk your life. Let your people do it. You stay here with me for a while. And let my father get you a new ship. It's the least we can do."

Day shook her head. "Thanks anyway. But these are loose ends I'd rather tie up myself." Like that rack-like gadget they use for torture. She was going to make sure it was never occupied again. And she had some scores to settle with the people who'd made her stay so memorable. She planned to ensure they got justice. "I'll pay you a visit at your school, after I'm finished on Taddayoosh. And as for the ship, well, I've gotten kind of attached to my Xannyk. It fits me."

"I can understand that," the Shameer's daughter said. "I feel the same way about this one. It feels friendly. All right! Have it your way. But let us help you on your return journey. I'll put a ship and crew at your disposal."

Day accepted the offer gratefully and turned back to the matter at hand, which was red and rich and rolled across her tongue beautifully. She'd call Auntie later, maybe tomorrow after a good rest. What the hell, she'd earned it and it wouldn't hurt those alien idiots to be held up one more day. It might even do them some good, make them more grateful to be invited into the Co-operative. Might even civilize 'em!

Or not. Who cared? Day wanted the Xannyk back, and not so she could return it. She figured Auntie owed her a couple of big ones now, and the Xannyk would be a good down payment. As the Shameer's daughter said, it was friendly. And it suited her.

"Can't your business wait?" Sharona asked, breaking into Day's reverie. "My father is coming and he wants to thank you in person."

Day shook her head. "Your father is the one person I would expect to understand about taking care of unfinished business," she said, though she agreed to meet the family on their homeworld for Sharona's birthday party, if she could get away. She smiled happily. She had no idea what would happen after she finished on Taddayoosh, but it didn't matter right then. Whatever it was, she felt confident that, between the gratitude of Auntie and the even more tangible gratitude of the Shameer, she'd be able to write her own ticket.

Maybe she'd even help Auntie train some new Supras, build a new batch of troubleshooters to get her off that merry go round once and for all. Who better to show them the ropes than her? It'd cost Auntie plenty, though. This time she was going to make sure it was all down in black and white, saved, printed, backed up, and archived, with airtight escape clauses. But that could wait.

She held out her glass for a refill.

## -The End-

Printed in the United States
35096LVS00002B/304-351